To M...

Hunt Heit Nera
1993

THE SPIRIT FLYER SERIES

# THE JOURNEY OF WISHES

## A Trip That Changed John Adam for Good

### JOHN BIBEE

*Illustrated by Paul Turnbaugh*

INTERVARSITY PRESS
DOWNERS GROVE, ILLINOIS 60515

*InterVarsity Press® is the book-publishing division of InterVarsity Christian Fellowship®, a student movement active on campus at hundreds of universities, colleges and schools of nursing in the United States of America, and a member movement of the International Fellowship of Evangelical Students. For information about local and regional activities, write Public Relations Dept., InterVarsity Christian Fellowship, 6400 Schroeder Rd., P.O. Box 7895, Madison, WI 53707-7895.*

*Cover illustration: Paul Turnbaugh*

*ISBN 0-8308-1207-5*

*Printed in the United States of America* ∞

*Bibee, John.*
'   *The journey of wishes/John Bibee.*
       *p.     cm.—(The Spirit Flyer series; 8)*
     *Summary: Sent to live with cousins on a farm during World War II,*
   *young John Adam finds himself on a strange journey, astride a rusty*
   *tractor bearing the "Spirit Harvester" logo.*
       *ISBN 0-8308-1207-5*
     *[1. Fantasy]  I. Title.   II. Series: Bibee, John. Spirit Flyer*
   *series; 8.*
   *PZ7. B471464Jo      1993*
   *[Fic]—dc20*
                                                                 93-8173
                                                                      CIP
                                                                       AC

16   15   14   13   12   11   10   9   8   7   6   5   4   3   2   1
05   04   03   02   01   00   99   98   97   96   95   94   93

*For Andrew Le Peau*

*Every writer
needs an editor
with insight, wisdom
and
deep vision*

# THE
# WISHES
# BEGIN
· · · · · · · · ·
# 1

There are wishes and there are wishes, as most children find out on their journeys. Some children follow wishes and dreams just like they would follow stepping stones in the middle of a dangerous swamp. They hop from wish to wish, hoping the next wish will take them to an even better one that will help them on their journey. Some wishes, like some stepping stones, are wobbly and weak and won't support a child, let alone a dreamer. These wishes stop in the middle of nowhere and leave you stranded and sinking on a private island of fear and doubt. But other wishes are more than mere stones. These wishes cut deep as solid rock to the core of all things. These wishes become as broad as roads and can hold an army of dreamers. There are wishes and there are wishes, as most children find out on their journeys. Some will lead us straight to the One who created our best and deepest dreams. But other wishes only leave us wishing for something more . . .

The summer Grandfather Kramar was eleven, he wished he were any place other than his Uncle Jacob's farm. But that wish, like many of his recent wishes, seemed to be in vain. He was so frustrated he did a very stupid thing that day, which started all the trouble.

John Adam Kramar, who went by the name Adam back then, was running away that Monday from his cousins, who were more than a little angry at him. As he ran out of the corn field and up onto the dirt road, he looked back over his shoulder, hoping he had lost them. He didn't stop for long. His cousins were a ways off, but they were getting closer. He turned and ran, leaving footprints on the hot dusty road.

As someone who had lived in a city all of his life, Adam felt like he was in the middle of nowhere being on his Uncle Jacob's farm. Not only was the farm a horrible place to spend the summer, he was also doing the hardest work of his life in what had to be the hottest weather in history. Summertime was supposed to be a time for fun, but he had decided they didn't know what real fun was like on the farm. Everything was work, from sunup to sundown. And since it was so hot, he was sure that any day he would just melt right down into a puddle of ooze just like a stick of butter left out in the sun.

His cousins, on the other hand, seemed to like all the work and sweat. They actually smiled and joked as they worked in the hot sun. But not Adam. He was at war with the work, the farm and now his cousins too.

In a way, Adam was at war because of another war. The whole country was at war in those days. After Japan bombed Pearl Harbor, the United States started fighting Japan and Germany. The war changed everyone's life. First, Adam's father had gone off to fight in Europe. He was a pilot and knew how to fly airplanes. At the beginning of the summer, his mother, a nurse, had also gone overseas to England to work in a military hospital. His older sister, Thelma, went to live with their Aunt Ida who worked in an airplane factory in Seattle. His parents had decided that the best thing for Adam was to live and work on his uncle's farm until the war was over.

The whole situation was a disaster as far as Adam was concerned. He had complained and griped from the day he had gotten off the train at the station in Centerville, which was the closest town to Jacob Kramar's farm. His cousins, in turn, didn't like the idea of Adam living with them. They called him lots of names like City Boy, Sleepyface, Scrawny and Lazy. They made fun of him because he hated to get out of bed in the morning while it was still dark and start the chores, like milking the cows and feeding the other animals.

They also made fun of him because he was thin. All his cousins were strong and husky from years of hard work and hearty meals. They acted like he was a weakling and laughed at him when he couldn't keep up with the chores. Adam kept wishing that somehow, some way, he could leave the farm and go back to his old home and be with his old friends. His friends didn't call him names or act like he was stupid or weak.

No matter what he wished, he was stuck on the farm. Each passing day added frustration to frustration. He finally got so angry that he decided to fight back. But his plan wasn't turning out the way he expected. His cousins were chasing him with surprising determination. They were clear across the big corn field when they saw him. So Adam had a good head start. But they had their bicycles and Adam was on foot. He knew he had to think of something quick if he was going to get away.

Adam ran as fast as he could down the old country road. Part of him wanted to go back and explain so his cousins would understand. But another part of him was too angry to talk.

"I don't owe them one ounce of explanation," Adam hissed to himself as he ran. "They're the ones being unfair. They're all a bunch of jerks."

His anger made him run faster. His steps left little clouds of dust each time his feet hit the ground. He looked over his shoulder and kept running. He didn't see the other boys yet, but they would be closing in. He glanced back over his shoulder again. They weren't in sight. He stopped to catch his breath.

"I wish I were someone else," Adam muttered to himself. "Why does all the bad stuff have to happen to me? I'd give anything to be anyone else and anywhere else than this stupid farm. If wishes were horses I'd ride, I guess."

He sighed in disgust, took a deep breath, and then began trotting down the road. The July sun was burning extra hot that day, and he was soaked in sweat.

"Maybe they gave up," he said to himself. He rounded a curve in the road and almost fell over as he stopped. Somebody was lying in the middle of the dusty road, right in front of a bridge that crossed the Sleepy Eye River. Adam stared at the body. He wondered whether the person was hurt or maybe even dead. For a moment he forgot about his cousins chasing him. He took a step toward the body to investigate when suddenly it moved. Adam froze.

A boy sat up in the road and jumped to his feet. He dusted off his clothes and smiled as he looked at the startled face of Adam Kramar. "Didn't mean to scare you," the boy said, still knocking off the dust. "But you're in big trouble and naturally I'm here to help. You wished, and I came back."

"But . . . but . . . " was all that Adam managed to stammer. "You . . . you look just like me. Are you a relative or something?"

The other boy grinned, but it wasn't a happy grin. Adam blinked. The boy looked like his reflection. He wore the same shirt, pants and shoes. He even seemed out of breath, as if he'd been running too. Yet something about him was different, as if he weren't quite normal. In fact, Adam was sure this wasn't a normal boy at all. For a moment, he thought he could see right through the boy.

"Am I just seeing things?" Adam wondered. He rubbed his eyes. "Is this person real?"

"Of course I'm real," the boy answered, as if reading Adam's thoughts. "You thought you got rid of me. But deep down I am you. I'm the one you wish to be, instead of the pathetic little coward you're acting like now by running away."

The boy who looked like Adam began to laugh. He kept on laughing and laughing so hard that it was beginning to make Adam angry. This kid, whoever he was, didn't seem to care whether or not he hurt Adam's feelings.

"Stop that!" Adam blurted out.

"Stop that!" the boy mimicked.

"Who are you?" Adam demanded.

"I'm your best friend, stupid. I can get you out of this jam too."

"How can you do that?"

"You have to trust me completely, and do what I say," the boy said seriously.

"Why should I trust you?"

"Who else are you going to trust?" the boy asked with a cynical smile. "You have to trust yourself because that's all you've got. You may think you've got friends, but you don't. Those Three Kings say they're with you, but if they were helping you, why are you stuck on this stupid farm? Now you're in big trouble, and you're about to get caught. Do you want to listen or not?"

"Why do you look like me?" Adam asked.

"Like I said, I am you, stupid! I'm the person you'd be if you had the guts to do things yourself. Only I wouldn't get caught like you're about to if you don't quit yakking. Now here's the plan. You leave the pet to give them a little scare. Then throw what they want in the river and run into that forest over there. Find the big tree and climb up as fast as you can. They'll never see you."

"What are you talking about?" Adam demanded. "What pet?"

"This pet, stupid." The boy reached inside his shirt and pulled out his hand. Adam jumped back. The boy was pulling out the biggest, longest, blackest snake Adam had ever seen in all his eleven years. Hand over hand he pulled and yanked until the serpent hit the road. The snake's head rose up into the hot July air. The black tongue flicked out in Adam's direction. Adam took a step backward. He had never seen a snake quite like that one lying in the road.

The snake rose up higher, its head swaying in the air. Adam watched it carefully. On the throat of the serpent was a strange marking: a white circle with a white X inside. The circled white X looked vaguely familiar to the boy, but he couldn't remember where he'd seen it before. He was sure he hadn't seen it on a snake, since he would have remembered that.

"Now follow the plan, stupid," the boy who looked like Adam said. "Throw this pet at them, toss the goods into the river and run to the forest. When you reach the big tall tree, climb up and we'll get you out of this mess you're in. Not only that, maybe we'll get back to the city where we belong."

"You can help me move back to the city?" Adam asked.

"Of course I can. I'm your best friend. I know what you want. You want to go back to the city and get out of this hick farm-boy country, right?"

"That's right."

"Then you'll need this." The boy reached inside his shirt and pulled out a small shiny black box about four inches long and three inches wide. The shiny sides of the box seemed to move and dance in the light. Adam leaned closer for a better look. For some reason, Adam sensed that the mysterious little box was filled with the most valuable treasures that he could imagine.

"That little box holds all your best dreams." The boy winked and stuffed the box back inside his shirt.

"Let me have it." Adam stepped forward, his hands reaching out.

"Not yet," the boy replied with a sly smile. "First, you've got to get rid of your cousins. Just make sure you grab our pet by the tail with both hands and throw it as hard as you can, or else our plan might not work."

Adam looked on the ground. The snake hissed loudly as Adam leaned closer for a better look. The hard red eyes like two beads seemed to glow as the black serpent stared at Adam. The snake slithered softly closer.

"He doesn't look very friendly." Adam looked up. But the other boy was gone. Adam looked all around. The strange boy had disappeared into the air. Adam wondered how that was possible.

He didn't wonder for long because he heard noises in the distance behind him. He turned around. Down the road, six boys on bicycles were pedaling toward him. The boys saw Adam just as he saw them. They shouted and stood up on their pedals. They seemed to be moving awfully fast for kids riding bikes, but Adam knew why. In his fear, he forgot everything but the need to escape. He turned to start running, but his legs wouldn't move. He looked down. The long black snake was quickly wrapping itself around his legs, in and out and around and over. He lost his balance and began to fall.

Adam hit the dirt road hard. He tried to kick off the serpent, but the scaly reptile only squeezed tighter, making an odd jingling sound. Adam braced himself for a painful bite which he felt sure must be coming at any instant. Out of the corner of his eye he could see the group of boys riding closer.

"There he is on the ground," the boy in front yelled. He had bright red hair.

"He fell down."

"He's our prisoner now," shouted another.

"Look at the chains around his legs," shouted the boy with red hair.

Adam Kramar looked down at his feet. He blinked in surprise. The coils of the moving snake were now the moving links of a dark chain. Adam stared in disbelief.

"What in the world is happening to me?" he gasped, trying to free his entangled legs. But the more he moved, the tighter the chain felt. Adam reached down to pull on it. He pulled his hand back quickly as soon as he touched the first dark link. The chain was freezing cold, so cold it felt like it was burning. Adam thrashed his legs, but it did no good. The chain finally stopped moving. The dark links squeezed his legs as tight as the vise in the workshop back on the farm.

The boys on the bikes skidded to a stop on the dusty ground a few feet away from the captive boy. Adam stopped struggling with the unusual chain so he could look up. He tried to catch his breath. He wiped the sweat off his forehead. Six big balloon tires were pointing straight at him. The boys on the bicycles stared down. They didn't look at all friendly. They weren't even breathing hard or sweating, even though they had been riding their bicycles as fast as the wind.

"What are you going to do with me?" Adam asked in a shaking voice. He stared at the boys. They were all older than he was, except Benjamin Kramar, who was ten.

"You know what we want," the boy with red hair said evenly. At sixteen Reuben was the oldest.

"But I don't have it," Adam spat out.

None of the boys said anything. They looked at each other silently.

"Liars usually get caught in their own lies," Reuben replied. Adam looked at their angry faces.

"Thieves get caught in their own traps." Simon was the second oldest. He squinted as he looked down on the trapped boy. "You know what we want. I think you better give back what you stole from us so we can all get back to work."

"But I didn't steal anything," Adam Kramar lied. The chain on his legs suddenly squeezed tighter and the boy cried out.

Reuben got off his bicycle. He knocked down the kickstand of the old red bike. He patted the seat. On the side of the bike, in flowing white letters, were the words *Spirit Flyer*. On the middle bar below the handlebars were three golden crowns linked to each other. A horn, an old light, a gear shift lever and a mirror were attached to the handlebars. A little metal generator shaped like a bottle was attached to the frame by the rear tire.

Adam stared at the old red bicycle with suspicion and disgust. The whole reason he was in trouble now was those stupid old bicycles, he thought. He would have gotten away if his cousins hadn't been on the bikes.

"We want it back right now." Reuben's green eyes were very serious.

"If you help me get this chain off, I can help you," Adam said feebly. "I can't even move with this thing on me. And it hurts like crazy."

"It's your chain." Reuben bent over and pointed at one of the links. "See, your name is right there, on every single link."

"What?" the boy asked. He bent over and squinted down at the chain. On every single dark link, his name was stamped in the metal, just like Reuben had said. And there was other smaller writing on the metal links, too small for Adam to read.

"I thought this thing was supposed to be gone," Adam said in a confused voice.

"If you're wearing the chain, it's because you asked for it." Jude Kramar was fourteen and the third oldest brother. He almost seemed to look at Adam with pity.

"The kings have freed you, but you can choose to return to the chains and act like a slave again," Reuben added.

"But only a real idiot would do something that dumb," Simon said. "And only some city-boy idiot would steal the key to the tractor. Now give it back."

"Don't call me a city-boy idiot," Adam spat out. He reached in his pocket and slowly pulled out the old worn tractor key. He held it up so they could see it. With a smile on his face, he threw the key over the bridge toward the Sleepy Eye River. In the same motion he reached down to yank the chain on his legs. As soon as he touched the links, it was a serpent again. In fear and disgust, he grabbed it by its tail and

flung the snake in the direction of his cousins, who were already running to rescue the key.

The snake hit the road and reared up. Benjamin Kramar aimed the headlight of his old red bicycle at the swaying serpent. Adam didn't wait to see what happened. He ran off the road and crossed a ditch.

"Get him!" Reuben yelled. "And get that key!"

Adam hopped over a barbed wire fence. He ripped the cuff of his jeans and fell. But he was up in an instant and running across the field toward the woods. His eyes opened wide when he saw the strange boy who looked like him standing at the edge of the forest waving for him to come.

Adam heard the voices shouting behind him. He ran faster. When he hit the row of trees, the strange boy looked very pleased.

"Come on," the boy said. "I know where they'll never find us." The boy ran ahead of him into the forest.

Adam didn't stop to ask questions. Without looking back he ran after the boy until he too disappeared among the tall trees.

# UP
# A DEAD
# TREE
· · · · · · · · ·
# 2

Adam ran through the forest following the mysterious boy. Though he heard the shouting voices of his cousins, he was afraid to look back. Besides, he was afraid he would lose sight of the odd boy he was following. His strange guide moved so quickly through the trees and underbrush that nothing seemed to slow him down. Adam wished he could run that fast.

"He's like a ghost or something," Adam panted, trying to keep up. "A very fast ghost."

"This way, this way!" the boy paused and shouted back to Adam. Then he was off again like a gust of wind. No matter how hard he ran, Adam never could seem to close the gap between him and the boy.

Before he knew it, the trees got taller and taller as the whole forest grew dark and dense. Adam was running fast when he tripped on a rotten log. He flew forward and hit the moist, leafy dirt of the forest floor. He gasped, spitting out black dirt and rotten leaves. He drew in big lungfuls of sweet, damp air as he lay on the forest floor, trying to catch his breath. Then slowly, his chest heaving, he raised his head and pushed up with his arms.

The forest was very dark and quiet and more than a little scary. Adam had never seen such tall ancient trees. For a moment it reminded him of the forests of fairy tales where little boys and girls get lost and taken away by horrible witches or wild creatures and beasts.

"Where am I?" Adam wondered. He looked around. He could still hear shouts in the distance, which he assumed were the voices of his cousins. Instead of fearing discovery, he almost wished he would be found. All the trees looked the same, their tall branches blocking out the sun. No birds sang. He couldn't even hear the buzzing of any insects. As he looked around, he realized that he didn't really know where he was or how far he had come from the road. He began to realize that he might be lost. Adam peered apprehensively around the dark woods.

"Over here," a voice called. Adam jerked his head around and walked in the direction of the sound. He looked and looked again.

"You're getting closer," the voice said and then laughed. Adam felt his face turn red. Why couldn't he see that boy? He walked near a huge tree. Adam marveled at its size. It was easily four times as big around as the other trees, old and gray and tremendously tall. As he gazed up the large trunk in wonder, he saw the boy sitting on one of the lower branches. The boy had the same crooked grin on his face. This time Adam was sure he could see through the boy.

"What took you so long?" the boy asked.

"I fell over a log," Adam said.

"Kind of clumsy for your age, aren't you?"

"Hey, I got here," Adam said angrily.

"Don't get your nose bent out of joint." The boy grinned. "The others will see you if you don't follow me up this tree."

Adam looked all around. He could still hear distant voices in the dark woods. Once again, he felt the desire to be found, not to be further lost from his cousins.

"But if they find you, you'll be in big trouble," the boy above him said. "You must be stupid or chicken to want to go back."

"I'm not chicken!" Adam protested. He opened his mouth to say more when he realized that the strange boy who looked like him had known what Adam was thinking. Adam had only *thought* about going back. He had never said it out loud.

"Of course, I know what you're thinking, you idiot," the boy said. "Like I said earlier, I'm you. I'm the old Adam, the good ole Adam you used to be before they told you all those lies. I know they told you that you got rid of me when you got that stupid Spirit Flyer bike. But that was just one of the lies that they tell new kids like you. They think if you believe in the kings that you'll believe in anything. They tell you I'm a ghost now, dead and gone. But here I am. You can't get rid of me. If I'm a ghost, I'll haunt you until you let me be real again. You don't really change, like they say. That's nonsense. How can you become a new person? You look the same in the mirror as you did before, don't you?"

"Yes, I guess so," Adam said. "But they said you change inside, in your heart . . . that old things become new . . ."

"Baloney!" the boy said. "I've always been here, the same as ever. I'm no ghost boy. I'm the real you and the only you, the same as ever."

"Then who am I?" Adam asked. He looked down at his hands. He had wondered about the changes they said he would experience. The first time he had ridden his own Spirit Flyer it all seemed to be true. He had felt like a new and different person as he flew high and fast above the clouds on the old red bicycle. But so much had happened since then.

A lot had been good, but there were also things Adam didn't like or understand.

"You're confused, that's all," the boy said. "But I'm here to get you back on track and out of trouble—if you follow me. It'll be just like old times, you and me and no one else. They'll never find us up in this tree. It's a special place. Besides, if you follow me, I might give you this."

The boy showed him the box again, only this time it was the size of a shoe box. The dark sides of the box suddenly seemed to be full of light and moving pictures with hints of treasure or secrets inside. Adam leaned closer for a better look. His mouth fell open as he stared.

"This box has more treasure than you can imagine," the boy said softly. "It's got everything you ever wanted. It may seem small, but it grows when you really take hold of it and own it. Look."

The boy lifted the lid. Lights flashed and cool blue smoke rushed out as the ghostly boy reached inside the strange box. He pulled his hand out holding a peanut. Adam blinked in surprise. Following the peanut was the moist tip of the trunk of an elephant!

Adam was so surprised he almost fell over backward. The elephant trunk just kept coming and coming out of the box, sniffing and reaching for the peanut. The boy gave him the peanut and the trunk disappeared back into the box.

"Remember the elephant you fed at the zoo last summer?" the boy asked.

"That was one of the most fun days of my life," Adam nodded wistfully. "We all went to the zoo together."

"This box holds the best times, all right, and the best times to come. Now follow me before those guys catch you."

The boy took the mysterious box that danced with colors and light and shoved it under his shirt. He stood up on a thick branch and began to climb up in the tree. He climbed higher and higher, almost leaping from branch to branch. Adam, curious to see more, started up the tree after him. The old gray branches were easy to climb on. Something did seem unusual or different about the tree, but Adam didn't stop to think about it.

The peculiar boy was jumping and leaping up faster than a squirrel. He must be a ghost, Adam thought. Being in the branches did make him feel different somehow. Part of the feeling was the excitement of escape, the feeling of power in having outwitted the ones who were chasing him. But there was something more, a somewhat troubling feeling because he was out of bounds. He had done something wrong and was running away. Now he was following that path away, out further and further. And the higher he climbed, the more guilty he felt. He should never have stolen the tractor key to begin with, and he knew it. He felt ashamed and weak. He felt a surge of anger toward himself and his cousins.

"Don't worry about your stupid cousins," the ghost boy said. Adam had been so lost in his thoughts, climbing mindlessly higher, that he hadn't even noticed that the other boy had stopped.

"They just want to boss you around and tell you what to do because you're only a cousin, not a member of the family." The boy put the black shiny box on his knee.

Adam looked greedily at the strange box. When he looked at it, he forgot about his cousins and the bad feeling of doing something wrong. The ghostly Adam slowly tipped open the lid of the box about an inch. Smoke and light oozed from inside.

"If we go high enough in this tree, near the top, I can give you this box," the boy said.

"Why can't I have it now?"

"Since you've come this far, you've earned one thing," the other boy said. "I can return the beads that belong to you. They tried to take them away, but I kept them safe. I've been waiting for the right moment to give them back."

The ghostly boy reached into the box and pulled out a long string of golden beads. Each golden bead was about the size of a jawbreaker.

The little balls were attached to each other by a small, dark chain.

"What kind of beads are they?" Adam asked.

"Precious memories," the boy replied with a crooked grin. "They tried to steal them from you, but you hadn't really forgotten them. They'll make you strong if you hold onto them tight enough. They don't want you to be strong, but these will give you power. More power than you ever believed possible."

He dropped the beads down into Adam's upstretched hands. The string of beads at once seemed stragely familiar. Adam didn't know how or when, but he knew deep inside that he had held this string of beads before. The beads were heavy and hard. Adam thought they probably did hold some kind of mysterious power. His curiosity was growing each second he held them.

"Wear them like a necklace," the old Adam instructed.

"Like a necklace on a girl?" Adam protested.

"Don't worry," the old Adam said. "Since they're your beads, they're invisible to everyone but you. If you wear them, you'll be more like me, powerful and strong. Wear these and your wishes to get out of this rotten place will come true."

Adam wasn't sure what the boy was talking about, but his curiosity had grown until it he felt compelled to do what the ghostly Adam said. He took the string of beads. With trembling hands, he hung them around his neck.

There were dozens of the odd beads on the dark chain. He felt the smooth surface of one of the beads. As he rubbed it, the golden color came off, like tarnish, revealing a black metal ball. Yet Adam wasn't disappointed. He suddenly knew what to do. He rubbed the bead harder, like the boy in the fairy tale who rubbed the lamp that made the genie appear. In the dark shiny surface of the bead he saw a picture that began to move.

It was the day his mother had put him on a train to go stay with Uncle Jacob and his sons on the farm. She had left the next day for the coast.

Adam had cried bitter tears as the train pulled out of the station. He had felt angry and lonely and betrayed all at the same time. Rubbing the heavy bitter bead, he remembered his misery all over again.

"They want you to forget what they did to you," the boy said to Adam. "But it's not fair. Why should you forget? If you do, they will hurt you again. Don't be a fool and get hurt again."

"I won't." Adam firmly rubbed the bead. The gold glitter paint fell off his hands like dust. The sweet agony of the memory filled him as the dust fell away.

Without a word, the ghostlike boy began climbing again, higher up the tree, taking the mysterious box with him. Adam climbed after him. As he struggled to keep up, he noticed that the branches were getting thinner and weaker. Then, as he looked around, he noticed that there were no leaves on any of the branches. That's what had seemed different about the tree, he thought to himself. It was totally dead, leafless and lifeless.

As Adam pulled himself up to the next branch, he heard a slight cracking sound. For the first time he looked down. He sucked in his breath. The ground looked so far away it made him feel dizzy.

"Don't be such a city-boy chicken." The boy with the box was sitting out on the far end of a limb. He held up the mysterious black box. Once again the sides began to move and swirl and dance with lights. "Come out here and you can have the box."

Adam looked down as he edged out on the bare dead branch. He only traveled a few feet before stopping.

"Why can't you bring it to me?" Adam asked. The dead limb cracked and moaned. "I could die if I fell out of this tree."

"Every wish or dream costs something." The boy wore his crooked grin. "The danger is what makes it fun. Come on. It's almost within reach."

Adam looked at the box and licked his lips. He moved farther out on the branch. The air seemed especially still and quiet. The sides of the box seemed to dance even more brightly as he got closer. The branch groaned again. Adam took a deep breath. He lunged for the box and the limb cracked. He tried to turn back, but he was too late. The branch made a popping sound and snapped away. Adam screamed as he dropped through the air like a falling stone.

# THE
# BEADS AND
# THE KEY

· · · · · · · ·

# 3

**Adam dropped** through the air, crashing through one branch and then another. The dead wood broke apart like rotten toothpicks. Though the branches slowed his fall, he still was going down at a sickening speed. Adam clawed desperately for one branch and then another, but they all broke off in his hands.

"Help me," Adam begged. He reached out again for the next branch. His body jerked around and his arm felt like it would be wrenched out of its socket, but the branch held. He wobbled in the middle of the air, high over the forest floor. Still in pain, he pulled himself along the branch, inching over to the trunk of the tree.

Finally he reached the trunk. He gasped in great gulps of air, trying to catch his breath. He was shaking and almost crying. He held the trunk so tightly that it hurt. Adam was wondering what to do when he saw him, walking right through the air as easily as if he was walking on the ground.

A man came toward Adam. He wore brilliant white clothes, so brilliant that the boy had to squint. The man smiled. Adam rubbed his eyes and looked again, thinking he might just be seeing things because he had bumped his head when he fell and didn't realize it. The man walked closer with an air of mystery and power. Adam felt afraid yet somehow glad to see this person. The man stopped and looked quietly at the boy. Then he spoke.

"John Adam Kramar, you are going to go on a journey," the man announced. "This will be a dangerous journey for a boy. But it's your journey, and you will complete the task that you have been asked to do. You will learn to trust me. Once you learn to trust me, you won't be falling out of dead trees or listening to those who would try to destroy your life."

"What?" Adam asked. "Who are you?"

"You know who I am," the man said, smiling once again.

"I think I do," Adam said. "You're the Prince of Kings. I saw you when I got my Spirit Flyer. But I didn't think I'd ever see you again. I thought you left me, like everyone else."

"I'm always with you," the man said. "I've always been with you. Even before you were born, I saw you sitting in this tree, trying to run away from your cousins because you stole the key to the tractor."

"You know about that?" Adam asked softly. He looked down at the branch feeling embarrassed and exposed.

"I know everything about you," the man said simply. "I know that you hate living on the farm. I know that you and your cousins argue and fight. I know you, John Adam Kramar, more than you know yourself. I know about your plan to run away if you get the chance. You've been getting train schedules and planning a route."

"You know that too?" Adam looked up with surprise. At first he was amazed, then he felt even more guilty because this person seemed to know all of his secrets.

"I know the heavy, bitter beads you carry around your neck. I know the misery they hold."

"What are they?" Adam asked.

"You'll understand in time," the man replied and smiled. "You aren't ready to give them up yet. You aren't ready because you still don't trust me."

"Trust you?" Adam muttered.

"If you knew me, you would trust me," the man said simply. "If you trusted me, you wouldn't chase after black boxes that promise gifts that are only made of dead things, things that would destroy you."

"But you don't understand," Adam protested. He suddenly reached up and held one of the heavy beads in his fingers. He rubbed it and felt the sweet bitterness. He began to feel sorry for himself all over again. "You don't know what it's like to live here. It's awful. They treat me like a slave. Work, work, work—that's all I ever do. It's summer. Most people have fun in the summer. But not these guys. All they do is chores, chores and more chores. They get up before dawn to milk cows. Then later we have to milk them all over again until it's almost dark. And that happens every day. You would think a cow would at least take Saturdays and Sundays off. I haven't had a good night's sleep since I got here."

The man looked at the boy and smiled. Adam saw him smiling and began to feel more angry.

"You don't understand," Adam added. "They call me names. They never let me drive the tractor. They treat me like a child or an idiot."

"Or a thief?" the man asked, still smiling.

"I was just trying to teach them a lesson," Adam said defiantly. "They don't know who they're messing with."

"And who are they messing with?" the man asked pleasantly.

"Well, . . . uh, I don't know, but I'm not their slave, I'll tell you that much. I'm somebody. I'm not just some kid from the city. They think I'm a dope, but I'll show them."

"You will show them." The man still smiled. "Only it won't be the way you think right now. You'll show them what I've given you, not the mere boasts of a boy but the power of the kings and the gifts of true life."

"What?" Adam asked in surprise. He assumed the man was being sarcastic at first, trying to kid him, or pull his leg. Adam reached for the heavy beads around his neck. He rubbed one, seeking its comfort. Suddenly he was sure the Prince was just teasing him. The thought made Adam bristle with anger. "You're just trying to fool me or make fun of me, like my cousins."

The Prince of Kings seemed very serious. The way he looked deep into Adam's eyes made Adam feel uncomfortable and then ashamed. The boy realized that deep down he didn't really believe or trust the Prince of Kings very much at all. Knowing that the Prince knew this sad truth made Adam feel very uneasy in his presence.

"I like you, John Adam," the man said gently, hearing the boy's thoughts. "That's why I've chosen you to go on a journey, a rather dangerous journey. In fact, you've already begun."

"But going on a journey where?" Adam asked angrily. "This is the third time you've told me and I still don't understand."

"You're forgetting your key," the Prince said. "Your key opens the door of your deepest and best wishes. Your key opens the doors to the riches of my kingdom. The key is a gift, but you must use it."

"What key?" Adam asked, feeling himself getting even angrier.

"The key I gave you when you became a part of my kingdom." The man pointed at the boy's chest. Adam looked down. He saw the heavy dark beads hanging around his neck. But underneath, hanging on a thin golden chain, was a golden key. Adam reached up and held it in his right hand.

While he was holding it, the Prince reached out and touched Adam's forehead. The instant he was touched, the boy's eyes were opened. Adam jerked back. Right in front of him, he saw a scene unfolding in the air. Adam thought it was just like watching a movie down at the Bijou Theater in Centerville. But this scene was happening in front of his eyes in the middle of the air. He was doubly surprised because he saw himself in this strange movie.

"It's me!" he said in surprise.

"Look deeper," the Prince said seriously.

Adam saw himself above the grounds of a carnival midway. He was riding a big red tractor that flew through the air. He passed over a large banner that said *Fattooka's Fantastic Midway*.

"I'm on a tractor that is flying," Adam whispered.

"A Spirit Flyer Harvester," the Prince said. "Just watch."

Adam saw himself flying toward a big ferris wheel that seemed to be turning at an unusually odd angle. The ferris wheel swayed and rocked. Adam flew the tractor high over the ferris wheel. He could see faces of the people in the cars. They seemed to be afraid. Some of the faces looked familiar. The background behind the ferris wheel looked familiar too. A large building stuck up above the rest in the distance.

"I'm flying above the ferris wheel," Adam said. "And I think I've been to that place. It looks real familiar."

"That's the fairgrounds near Centerville," the Prince said. "That's the courthouse in the background."

"You're right! The fair and carnival is supposed to start there soon. Uncle Jacob was going to take all of us." The movie slowly faded from view. "But what does it mean?" Adam asked. "And how can a tractor fly?"

"It's a Spirit Flyer Harvester," the Prince replied plainly. "Wait until you are sent on the next part of your journey. When the time comes, go straight to your destination, John Adam Kramar. Don't look to the right or the left, but go where your Spirit Flyer leads you. Don't fight the spirit of the flight. Your enemy wants to distract you. But if you follow me and obey, you will escape the dangers and heartaches of the chain."

Adam thought of the chain of beads and let go of the key. With empty hands, he looked at the chain and the golden key hanging around his neck. He touched the dark beads. An old familiar feeling came rushing back. Instantly, Adam wondered if the Prince was telling him the truth.

"I'll have to think about all this stuff," Adam said slowly, still rubbing one of the beads. He looked at the mysterious golden key. "I guess I forgot that I even had that key."

"Your enemies would like you to forget everything about your new life in my kingdom. They want you to forget who you are and the gifts you've inherited in my name. The ghost slave lies to you whenever he can. The more you listen, the more he lies. Your enemies want you to return to their house of lies."

"House of lies?" Adam asked, feeling confused. The bead in his hand felt suddenly hot. He let go of it. The Prince smiled. For an instant, Adam's head felt clearer. He felt like he was understanding the words of the Prince.

"Your enemies want you to forget," the Prince repeated. "They only want you to remember what you were like before you met me. They don't want you to receive or use the gifts I've given you. They know that when you use my gifts, the old house of lies will be destroyed."

For an instant, Adam saw it like another movie. Before his eyes, an old, dark, spooky house was falling down. As the walls fell and boards splintered, Adam saw himself running out of the house. Other things came out of the house behind him. Dark, shadowy shapes flew out, like winged beasts and serpents. They looked like they wanted to hurt him. Adam suddenly felt afraid. He reached for the beads and rubbed one. The picture of the awful house was suddenly gone. Adam felt relieved not to see it, but deep inside he felt unsettled.

Adam held onto the string of bitter beads. He looked down at the golden key with sadness. Part of him wanted to hold it too. But deep down he knew he couldn't hold the heavy dark beads and the golden key at the same time. He hesitated for a moment but kept the bitter beads in his hand. He had held the beads so often they were like old friends. He had relied on them much more than the mysterious golden key. He trusted the familiar comfort the beads would bring if he rubbed them long enough.

The Prince looked concerned and sad. He stared at Adam in silence. He realized that the boy had made his decision. "I love you, John Adam Kramar. You will complete your journey. Then you'll trust me as much as you trust the ground you walk on. And when you trust me, you'll use the gifts I've given you as well."

The Prince's words hung in the air. He smiled once more at Adam and then slowly faded from view. Adam blinked in surprise. He sensed that the man hadn't really left, but only that he had disappeared from sight. Adam looked down at his chest. The golden key shimmered and then it too seemed to fade away. Only a faint outline remained. The boy grunted in disgust. He gripped the dark beads and rubbed them harder.

"Yak, yak, yak. I thought he'd never leave," a voice said behind him. "I'm glad you invited me back. You can't trust that guy. All he does is confuse you."

Adam looked around the trunk of the tree. The ghostly boy was sitting on the branch just above him, smiling with his crooked grin.

"How did I invite you?" Adam asked.

The ghost boy opened his mouth but didn't speak. He was looking off in the air behind Adam. The ghost boy looked concerned and frowned. "Better get out of here," the peculiar boy said suddenly. "See you later, alligator."

"What are you talking about?" Adam demanded. But the strange boy disappeared. "What's bothering him?" Adam asked out loud. He turned around to see what had scared the unusual boy. He jerked back. Off in the distance, six red bicycles were sailing right at him.

# AT THE SUPPER TABLE

· · · · · · · · ·

## 4

**Adam frantically** looked around for a place to hide. He quickly realized that the bare dead branches wouldn't hide a squirrel, let alone a boy. He started to climb down, but the ground was too far away. The bicycles shot forward in the air. Adam frowned when he saw the one in the lead was his cousin Reuben. All his cousins were right behind him. Reuben smiled triumphantly as he flew closer. Soon all six bikes were parked around the tree trunk, hanging high in the air.

"I knew we'd catch up to you," Reuben said confidently. "You can ride on the back of my bike back to the hay field."

Adam looked down the tree, wishing there was some way he could escape.

"Don't even think about trying to get away this time," Simon said. "You've already wasted enough time with your stupid prank."

"We got the key," his cousin Dan said, holding up the tractor key. "You had bad aim. It landed on the bank, not in the water."

"We need to get back," Reuben said. "You can ride on the back of my bike."

"Okay," Adam said reluctantly. He climbed slowly onto the back of the old red bicycle. He knew he had lost the battle, but he wasn't giving up, he told himself. "No matter what they do, they won't get the best of me," he thought.

"When Pop hears what you tried to do, I wouldn't want to be in your shoes." Simon had a bent smile. The other boys nodded eagerly.

Adam shrugged. He knew they couldn't wait to tell on him. He acted like he didn't care. He wouldn't let them see that he was afraid. But that's exactly how he felt as the boys began to pedal toward the hay field.

The rest of the afternoon, his cousins kidded him about what was going to happen when they got home. The more they talked the more uneasy Adam felt. The hot afternoon in the hay field dragged by more slowly than ever.

Adam was dead tired by the time they gathered around the big oblong table that night. Uncle Jacob, a tall, strong man, limped as he walked to his chair. His cousins had told Adam that their father had been in some sort of accident as a young man, and that had caused his limp. But no one knew what kind of accident it was because their father never told them. He wasn't a man who talked a lot. Nor did he raise his voice much, even if he was angry. He sat in his big chair at one end of the table. He stared at Adam for a moment but said nothing.

Adam cringed as he set down a big bowl of mashed potatoes. Mrs. Kramar, Benjamin and Adam continued setting out the plates of food. The older boys all watched quietly. They had told their father about the situation with the tractor key, and they wondered how he would respond.

Mr. Kramar said grace and they began to eat. He asked how many hay bales had been put up in the barn and how many had been left in the field.

They talked about news from Europe and the war. Carl Wethersby, a farmer's son from just across the county line, had been severely wounded in France, Mr. Kramar said. He had been wounded by a machine gunner's bullet. He had heard the news down at the feed store.

"I wish I could go over there and help out," Reuben said almost angrily.

"Enough people are dying already," his mother said softly. "The Army doesn't need you for another few years, and I hope it's over by then."

"I bet Reuben could take care of old Mr. Adolf Hitler and a bunch of those Nazis too," Dan said with a smile. "He's the best shot in the county. Everyone knows that."

"You're doing a good job here," Mr. Kramar said. "Besides, going hunting for squirrels for the stew pot isn't anything like combat. I hope none of you have to do that. All of us are contributing to the war effort by being good farmers. Soldiers have to eat."

No one said anything. All the boys knew stories about how their father had served in the Great War twenty years ago in France. He had been a good soldier and had medals and ribbons in a metal box in the closet. But he rarely talked about the war even though he had been an officer and hero. He would have gone to war a second time if it hadn't been for his bad leg and hip. He had tried, but the Army had turned him down and told him to be a farmer, that he had served enough as a soldier.

"I heard there was a problem in the hay field today." Uncle Jacob slowly turned to Adam. "What's your side of it?"

Adam looked down at his plate in silence. Everyone in the room was looking at him.

"Nothing," Adam said very softly.

"Nothing?" Mr. Kramar asked. "You ran off with the key to the tractor and tried to throw it in the river. Then you hid up in a tree, and you've got nothing to say?"

"No, sir, well . . . I mean, I never get to drive the tractor. I know how, but nobody lets me have a turn. Everyone else gets to drive but me, and it doesn't seem fair."

Adam gulped and shut his mouth. All of a sudden he felt like a whining baby. Tears were close and a lump was forming in his throat, which was even more embarrassing than having everyone staring.

"Your trip to the river and woods took over an hour," Mr. Kramar said evenly. "One hour each of seven workers means seven hours lost. That's about how long it will take you to clean out the chicken house the weekend we go to the fair in Centerville."

"Clean the chicken house?" Adam asked. "You mean by myself? No one will help me?"

"We'll give you the scoop shovel and the wheelbarrow," his uncle said.

"But the chicken house stinks something awful!" Adam protested. "I hate going in there even to get the eggs."

"It does stink pretty bad, and that's why it needs be hauled out and fresh floor put in." Mr. Kramar had a slight smile. "First you take out the old and then put in the fresh."

"But that will take hours!"

"About seven hours if you work hard and steady," his uncle said, nodding. "That's fair time to make up for what you lost today."

Adam opened his mouth to protest again but then stopped. He looked around the table. All the other boys were smiling. Cleaning out the chicken house was one of the worst chores on the farm.

"It's just not fair," Adam said feebly. "I get the worst jobs of anybody."

"All of us have cleaned the chicken house," his uncle replied.

"He just thinks he's too good to get his city-boy hands dirty," Simon said in disgust.

"I do not!" Adam shot back. "You just better watch—"

"Quiet! Both of you," Mr. Kramar said looking at Simon and then Adam. "Adam will clean the chicken house. And tomorrow, Adam will get a turn to drive the tractor part of the day. Do you hear me, Reuben?"

"Yes, sir," Reuben said flatly. The oldest boy didn't appear to be happy about the idea.

"You mean I really get to drive?" Adam asked, feeling more hopeful.

"You'll get your turn, and we'll see how you do," Mr. Kramar said.

"It's about time," Adam muttered.

"I've been keeping a secret." Mr. Kramar said with a smile. "We have a surprise tonight. Great Uncle Samuel is coming to visit. He has something he wants to talk to us about."

"Uncle Samuel? Tonight?" Reuben asked. All the other boys were suddenly very attentive. Everyone loved Uncle Samuel. He told wonderful stories about all sorts of things. He was old and wise and more than a little mysterious. He knew more about Spirit Flyers and the Three Kings than anyone else they knew.

"He can sleep in my bed," Dan said.

"No, let him stay in our room," Benjamin replied. "He stayed in your room last time. Daddy, make him stay with Adam and me."

"We'll let Uncle Samuel decide where to sleep," their father said with a smile.

"What's his business about?" Reuben asked.

"He didn't really say," his father said. "You know how he is. He can be downright secretive."

"And very strange," Mrs. Kramar added, getting up from the table. She wiped her hands on her apron. "For some reason, he didn't want us to tell you boys that he was coming by until the last minute. He's the oddest character in the whole family."

"But you love him too, don't you, Mama?" Benjamin asked.

"Of course I do," Mrs. Kramar said. "He's the one that married your father and me on our wedding day. But he's still a character."

"I've never met him." Adam frowned. "I've heard my parents mention him. He sounded kind of weird to me."

"How can you judge someone you've never met?" Dan bristled with contempt. "Is that another thing they do in the city?"

"Actually, Adam has met him," Uncle Jacob said. He turned to Adam. "You don't remember it, but I do. He was there the night you were born. I was there too. Uncle Samuel held you in his arms when you were no more than five hours old. He said he wanted to be there especially on the day you were born. He walked all over the old county hospital holding you and talking real softly. He seemed real interested in you."

"In me?" Adam asked.

"In him?" Dan asked with even more surprise. All the other boys looked at Adam suspiciously.

Mr. Kramar's eyes twinkled as he got up from the table. He pushed his heavy chair back in place.

"Now you boys help your mama with the dishes and get the evening chores done before you listen to the radio," Mr. Kramar said. "Leave the dishwater. Uncle Samuel will want to eat supper too."

"I have my own surprise to share too," Mrs. Kramar said with a smile.

"What is it, Mama?" Benjamin asked.

"You'll have to wait and see." Mrs. Kramar put a finger over her lips.

"I wonder why Uncle Samuel is coming here this time?" Simon asked Reuben.

"I can't believe he'd care a hoot about Adam," Dan said with envy.

"Maybe he can show him a special way to clean the chicken house," Simon said with a grin.

"Shut up," Adam grumbled and started clearing the plates. The other boys laughed and whispered as Adam carried a load of dishes to the sink. He tried to ignore them and their comments, but it wasn't easy. For once he was grateful to be doing the dishes because it helped him ignore his cousins. Soon he was up to his elbows in the sudsy dishwater, wondering about Uncle Samuel and why he was coming to visit.

The dishes were finally done and Uncle Samuel still hadn't arrived. Adam's cousins were gathered around the radio in the living room listening to Fibber McGee and Molly. Adam normally liked to listen too, but he felt like his cousins didn't want him around so he went outside.

The summer night was falling. A few stars twinkled in the dark blue sky. Adam wished he could talk to his sister. Or better yet, he wished his parents were home safe and sound so he wouldn't have to be afraid for them anymore. A cold feeling gripped his stomach suddenly as he thought of his father flying airplanes over enemy skies.

"I should just leave here," Adam thought bitterly. "I could run away tonight, and they wouldn't care if I was gone or not. They all hate me. And I hate them."

Just then, he heard the chug, chug chugging sound of a tractor in the distance. Adam liked the sound. But something seemed different about this sound. It wasn't coming from the road. Adam walked out into the yard to investigate. The sound was getting louder. The tractor seemed very close. But he still couldn't see it out on the road or by the barn. The chugging noise increased even more, almost as if it was on top of him. Adam looked up.

"Aaaaackkk!" Adam yelped when he saw a large tractor pass in front of the full moon. The big machine sailed through the sky, making a circle over the farmhouse. Adam watched with his mouth hanging open. The big tractor glided downward. Adam ran to the porch.

"Uncle Jacob, Uncle Jacob!" Adam yelled. His uncle came out on the porch.

"What's the matter?" his uncle asked.

Adam pointed to the yard as the big tractor chug-chugged down to the ground. It rolled to the front of the barn and stopped.

Uncle Jacob smiled widely. He patted Adam on the back. "Don't be afraid, son. That's just your Great Uncle Samuel."

# GREAT
# UNCLE
# SAMUEL
· · · · · · · · · ·

# 5

Uncle Jacob walked over to greet the visitor on the mysterious tractor. The two men shook hands and then went inside the barn. Adam hesitated before walking slowly over to the big red tractor. He touched one of the huge back tires. He looked at the tractor suspiciously. *Spirit Flyer Harvester* was painted in flowing white letters on the side.

"That's what the Prince called that tractor this afternoon," Adam whispered. "This is getting weird. I wish I could get out of here before things get really strange."

"You look like a boy on a real important journey," a deep voice said behind him. Adam turned around. A very tall, old man with a red beard was looking right at him. He was smiling. His green eyes were friendly, but very intense. Wild, bushy red eyebrows wiggled when he smiled. He was bald on top, but the sides of his head were covered with red and grey hair, though not as red as his beard. His nose was somewhat long and slightly crooked. The man leaned on a long wooden stick and continued to stare at Adam with his intense eyes. Adam wasn't sure what to say.

"Pardon me?" Adam asked.

"I can tell you're on an important journey, but I don't think you'll be leaving tonight," the man said. "Timing is everything when you take a trip. The best journeys are the ones that begin when you're ready, not just the times when you want to run away."

Adam gulped. Somehow the strange old man seemed to know that he wanted to run away. But how could he? He had never even seen this strange person before.

"I see you've met John Adam Kramar," Uncle Jacob said. "This is William's boy."

"We were just getting acquainted." Uncle Samuel smiled. "Of course, he's changed a bit since he was a baby." The old man looked at Adam and winked.

"We kept supper hot for you, Uncle Samuel. Come on inside. Everyone's waiting."

"I was hoping you'd say that," the old man said. "I've been thinking about Rachel's biscuits since I left my farm."

The two men walked to the house. Adam followed them. When they got on the porch, Uncle Samuel turned and looked at Adam carefully.

"I sure am glad to finally get to see William's boy here, growed up a bit now. When I saw you the first time, you didn't say much. Just gurgled, spat and cried louder than most any little baby I've seen."

"Oh." Adam wasn't sure how to react to the unusual old man. He was glad his cousins hadn't heard that remark.

"Yep, you sure made a ruckus when you hit the world, screaming at the top of your lungs to beat the band." The green eyes of the old man twinkled. "You let everyone in that hospital know that you had arrived. I could tell right then that people would always sit up and take notice of you. Your light won't be hid under a bushel. You're someone who's always going to stir things up so people pay attention."

"That's been true around here." Uncle Jacob nodded his head in agreement. Adam thought his uncle would then say something critical or tell him about the tractor key, but he didn't.

Adam wasn't sure what to think or say. He followed the men inside. Everyone cheered and jumped up when they saw Uncle Samuel. They made the old man sit at the end of the kitchen table and began bringing him food. Adam stood back and watched quietly. Simon gave him a dirty look, but the others were too excited that Great Uncle Samuel had come to visit. He seemed to be their favorite person in the whole family.

As he ate, Adam could tell why. Uncle Samuel told jokes and fascinating stories. Apparently he was also some kind of inventor too, besides being a farmer and retired schoolteacher. For a tall man, he didn't eat much, which was just as well because he liked to talk more than eat. He knew all the boys by name and asked each one different questions. He knew all about them and what they liked and didn't like. Each boy loved the attention.

"I'm playing tuba in the school band, now, Uncle Samuel," Jude said proudly. "Mr. Johnson says I'm one of the best he's ever heard."

"Well, I'm not surprised." Uncle Samuel smiled. "We all know what a blowhard you are. Of course, you have to blow hard to blow a great big tuba."

The other boys laughed. Jude smiled, enjoying the kidding from the others.

As Uncle Samuel talked, Adam felt himself growing jealous that the old man knew so much about his cousins. He began to wish that Great Uncle Samuel would like him as much as he liked them.

"Why did you come to visit, Uncle Samuel?" Simon asked. All the boys suddenly got quiet. None of them had heard the reason for his visit, though they were sure he had one.

"Well, I'll tell you boys," the old man said slowly, "after I eat." The boys all groaned and Uncle Samuel smiled. His sparkling green eyes seemed full of secrets and surprises.

"Have you invented any new stuff lately?" Benjamin asked eagerly.

"I've been working a lot with the new recycling programs the government has instituted," the old man said. "And since I'm a gardener, I've gone to many of the local towns to talk about gardening. I even went to St. Louis to help people start their own gardens."

"They call them victory gardens in town," Benjamin said. "Of course, we just call ours a regular garden like it's always been."

"It is our regular garden," Mrs. Kramar said. "The war hasn't changed everything, though it sure has changed a lot of things."

"In Centerville they are recycling lots of stuff for the war effort too," Reuben said. "They take old tires and inner tubes, newspapers, and all kinds of metal. They said they can make four hand grenades out of an old shovel. We save all our tin cans, and everything made out of bronze or brass, like old padlocks."

"They even want us to bring bacon grease and old stockings." Mrs. Kramar smiled. "I'm glad they can find a good cause for these things instead of just throwing them away. It would make sense if we'd recycle more things all the time, not just when there's a war. I think too much goes to waste."

"Not one of your biscuits will go to waste while I'm around!" Great Uncle Samuel joyfully picked up the last one from the plate. He cut it open with a knife and buttered it carefully.

"Save a little room for dessert," Mrs. Kramar said. "Since I knew you were coming, I made our end-of-the-month cake." The boys around the table cheered at the announcement. Benjamin jumped up.

"Is that the surprise, Mama?" he asked.

"Yes. And not only that. Reuben, you and Simon can make ice cream too, since there was leftover sugar. There's a new block of ice in the icebox that you can use."

"Great!" Reuben loved making the ice cream almost as much as he loved eating it.

The end-of-the-month cakes were indeed special because sugar was one of the many rationed items since the war had started. Once a month they bought sugar with ration coupons and money. Mrs. Kramar kept most of the sugar for the family pantry. The rest she gave in equal amounts to each child. Each person, including Adam, had a Mason jar with his or her name on it. Mrs. Kramar said they could use their sugar as quickly or as slowly as they wanted. Most of them put it on their oatmeal in the morning very sparingly. If there was enough sugar left at the end of the month, everyone pitched in and she made a cake for the whole family. Having enough for cake and homemade ice cream was a double treat.

Uncle Jacob and Great Uncle Samuel walked into the living room and sat down in front of the fireplace to talk. The other kids rushed around to get ready for the ice cream. Benjamin put clean bowls and plates on the table. Adam counted out the correct number of forks and spoons. He then followed Benjamin outside to watch the ice cream being made. Reuben and Simon were in charge of the ice cream freezer. Adam sat in the porch swing and watched from a distance. Benjamin begged to try his hand at turning the ice cream.

While Benjamin turned the handle, Adam watched enviously. He would have liked to try too, but he figured his cousins wouldn't let him. "What if I spilled it or something?" Adam thought to himself. "They'd never let me forget that for a million years."

He rubbed his hands together. He looked down and was surprised to see the shadowy, round misery beads clutched inside his hands. He looked quickly around, wondering if the ghost boy was nearby.

"They don't want you with them," he heard a voice say. Adam whirled around. The porch was empty, but he could still hear the boy's voice. "You should just go upstairs and go to bed. This family doesn't want you. Go to bed and leave them alone. They'll resent you even more if you eat any of their precious cake or ice cream."

"Maybe you're right," Adam said softly. Once again he felt a heavy wave of loneliness wash over him. "Maybe it would just be simpler to go upstairs and read or just go to sleep."

Adam rocked slowly back and forth in the swing, lost in his sad thoughts. Suddenly, his cousins hollered in glee because the ice cream was done. They all ran inside. Mrs. Kramar was cutting the cake with a long knife.

"I have a piece almost ready for you, Adam." She carefully cut through the white frosting.

"I'm not really hungry," Adam lied. "I'm going up to bed, I guess."

"More for us then!" Simon said.

"Are you feeling sick, son?" Uncle Jacob asked with concern.

"I don't know. Maybe I'm just tired," Adam replied. He felt more and more lonely. Seeing the whole family gathered in the living room made him sad, wishing he could be with his own family. Great Uncle Samuel stood in the corner, leaning on his walking stick. He looked at Adam carefully.

Adam turned and walked slowly up the stairs. With each step, he felt more sad and hopeless. He didn't understand why, except that he missed his family. He brushed his teeth and sat down on the bed. Downstairs, everyone was laughing and talking and having a good time. Everyone was having a good time except him. Great Uncle Samuel was telling jokes again, but Adam couldn't quite hear all the words, so none of them made sense. He lay on the bed, trying to block out their voices. Then he heard someone calling his name.

"Adam, come downstairs!" It was Uncle Samuel calling him.

Adam reluctantly walked downstairs. Everyone was in the kitchen around the big table. Great Uncle Samuel stood near the sink. His walking stick was lying on the kitchen floor right at his feet.

Everyone turned and stared as Adam walked in. He wasn't sure why they were looking at him in such an odd manner.

"Let me try again, Uncle Samuel," Simon asked. The older boy looked flustered. He got up from the table, bent down and took hold of the walking stick. He strained to pick it up, but couldn't lift it. He tried three times, and each time his muscles bulged and his face turned red, but the stick stayed on the floor as if it was nailed down. Uncle Samuel smiled.

"Adam, you're just in time," Great Uncle Samuel said. "And you're the only one left."

"Only one left?" Adam asked.

"I came here to borrow a boy," the old man said. "I had an idea of which boy to take with me, but I wanted to be sure. It's not really a contest. It's more a matter of the Three Kings' choice. Will you come over here and pick up my staff?"

"Pick up your staff?" Adam asked. "You mean your walking stick?"

"That's right."

"Isn't it nailed down or something? Simon couldn't pick it up," Adam said. "Is there some kind of trick?"

"It's not a trick," the old man said. He bent down and picked up the walking stick with one hand. He turned it around like a drum major twirling a baton and then set it back down on the floor.

"Why don't you try?" The old man had a glint in his eyes. He pulled on his red beard with his long thin fingers.

"I guess I can try," Adam said, still not quite understanding. He walked across the room. He looked down at the wooden stick. He bent over, took hold of it with both hands and lifted it. The stick wasn't at all heavy. It was as easy as lifting a shovel or a garden rake. He stood up straight, holding the long stick.

All around the table, the other boys stared at Adam with open mouths. Uncle Jacob smiled.

"How can he be the one?" Simon asked indignantly. "There has to be some mistake."

Simon jumped up from the table and walked over to Adam. He grabbed the wooden stick and yanked. Adam let go. The stick fell like a stone straight to the floor, jerking Simon's arms down with it.

"Ouch!" Simon yelled as the stick hit the floor. He straightened up and immediately sucked on his thumb, which had gotten pinched. He glared at the stick and then glared at Adam suspiciously.

"Pick it up again, Adam," Benjamin said. Adam shrugged his shoulders. He reached down and picked up the stick just like before. The wooden staff didn't seem to weigh any more than a few pounds. He looked at it carefully. The gnarled wood was worn and shiny smooth. A bright brass tip was on the bottom of the stick. Near the top, three golden crowns were set into the wood. Adam rubbed his finger over the three crowns.

"I thought Adam was the one chosen for the task, but I wanted to make sure," Great Uncle Samuel patted Adam on the back. "It looks like you're going to go on a journey, my boy."

"A journey?" Adam asked.

"Why does he get to go?" Simon demanded. "I'm older. And besides, he'll mess everything up. I can't believe the kings would want him when they could send me instead."

"Everyone has their share to do in the Kingdom," Great Uncle Samuel said seriously. "As it says in *The Book of the Kings,* those who are in the Kingdom are like a body. We each have our place of responsibility, but we aren't all eyes or hands or feet. The hands don't do the work of the eyes, and the feet don't try to see. Adam was chosen before he was born for the tasks he's been called to do. And it was the kings who chose him. He didn't choose himself."

"That's sure the truth," Adam muttered. "I don't even know what's going on. What are you talking about? This is the fourth time I've heard about going on some journey. I still don't understand."

"The fourth time, son?" Uncle Jacob asked. "When did you hear about it before?"

"He told me a few times before I moved here," Adam said simply. "It was after my dad left, but I was still with my mom. It happened around the time I woke up, two mornings in a row. I didn't say anything to anyone because I just thought it was some weird dream or something. I saw that guy, the one they call the Prince of Kings, in the dream and he told me about a special journey I would go on. Then today when I was up in that big dead tree, I saw the Prince again. He told me about a journey again and even said it was dangerous. I thought coming to live here was what he meant the first two times. I still don't understand any of this stuff."

"Your journey began before you were even born," Great Uncle Samuel said. "The kings have always known the things you will accomplish, the places they will send you. That's true for all of us."

"But what journey is he talking about if I'm already on a journey that started before I was born?" Adam looked confused.

"There's a special task you've been called to do," the old man said mysteriously. "I know I'm supposed to help you get ready. But I don't know all the details. I have a few ideas."

"Uncle Samuel always has lots of ideas," Reuben said with a smile. The other boys nodded. They all looked at Adam enviously.

"I think this particular part of your journey is like a side trip on a longer trip," the old man said. "But it's an important side trip, and as the Prince of Kings said, there must be an element of danger."

"But what about cleaning the chicken house?" Adam asked. "I can't just leave here, can I? What about my chores and putting up the hay?"

"You won't leave for a few days," Uncle Jacob said with a smile. "You boys should be able to finish putting up the hay in the bottom today. Besides, tomorrow is your day to drive the tractor, remember?"

"Sure," Adam said slowly. "I don't want to miss out on that."

"We've had a long day," Uncle Jacob said. "Everyone to bed. Morning comes early on a farm."

All the children groaned. Great Uncle Samuel stayed in the kitchen to talk more with Jacob as the boys went upstairs.

"Why should Uncle Samuel want him?" Simon murmured to Reuben. Adam avoided their angry stares and walked quickly into Benjamin's room and got ready for bed.

He pulled the covers almost over his head. He knew his cousins were angry. He thought about the walking stick and Great Uncle Samuel and the strange talk about a journey. He closed his eyes, still wondering. Soon he was wondering in his dreams.

# DRIVING
# THE
# TRACTOR
· · · · · · · ·
# 6

The hot July Wednesday seemed hotter than usual in the hay field that day. Adam was itching to drive the tractor but itching even more from the hay. Everyone's shirt was soaked with sweat by ten o'clock in the morning, and it just got hotter and stickier as the day wore on. Adam tried not to complain because he knew the other boys would say something mean about him being from the city or being weak or lazy.

Adam did ask Reuben when it would be his turn to drive the tractor. They usually took turns, once in the morning, after lunch, and in the middle of the afternoon. Reuben finally said Adam could drive in the afternoon. At first Adam was angry because he would have to wait, but then he realized it would be the hottest part of the day and he would be driving, not stacking the itchy hay bales. Also, the last person driving got to take the tractor home if the wagon was full and the hay ready for the barn.

Gasoline was rationed for the rest of the war, the government said, and not easy to come by. Farmers like the Kramars were allowed more gasoline because they needed it on the farm. But Mr. Kramar insisted on no unnecessary trips from the field to the house so they could save fuel.

Finally, Reuben called for the afternoon break. Adam drank cool water from the big galvanized water cooler they kept under the shade tree at the end of the field.

"It's my turn to drive, right?" Adam asked. "I know how to use the controls, so you don't have to show me."

"Not so fast," Reuben said firmly. "I'm going to have Dan drive for an hour, then you."

"But I should get to drive the rest of the afternoon," Adam insisted.

"Look, Mr. Hotshot. Uncle Samuel may have chosen you to go on some strange journey with him, but out here, I'm still the boss," Reuben replied. He smiled at his brothers, and they grinned back. "You aren't as special as you think you are, City Boy."

"But your dad said you had to let me have my turn to drive," Adam protested. He could feel his face getting hot. "Besides, I never said I was special."

"Well, you aren't any better than the rest of us," Reuben said evenly. "You will have a turn in about an hour."

"But that's not fair," Adam insisted. "The person in the afternoon always gets to drive until quitting time."

"That's not how we're doing it today," the oldest boy said. "Now let's get back to work."

The other boys smiled and nudged each other as they headed back out into the sunny field. Dan got up on the tractor and started it. Adam climbed angrily back on the hay wagon.

"This isn't fair at all," he muttered to himself. He felt like kicking a hay bale and he did. Then he was sorry because even though hay is soft, it's still very heavy and firm when it's tightly baled. His foot burned with pain. The other boys smiled but said nothing as he limped across the wagon.

Adam worked without speaking for the next hour. The tractor went up and down the rows, as they picked up the bales of hay. The boys on the wagon talked about the war and the bombing raids on London. Adam wished they wouldn't mention it since he thought about his mother being over in England. In her last letter she insisted that she was away from the city in a safe hospital, but Adam wasn't convinced. His mom said each night they had what they called blackouts, which meant they covered up all the lights inside houses and buildings so that if enemy planes came at night, they couldn't see where to bomb. But even with blackouts, the German planes were causing a lot of destruction.

Reuben told Dan to stop as they reached the end of the field near the water cooler. The boys all ran for a drink. Adam gulped in the fresh water. The boys kept talking about the war and local people they knew who were fighting overseas.

"I wish the war would be over," Adam said out loud. "My mother wrote that she thinks the Allies will start taking ground back soon and that we'll win."

"What does your dad think?" Simon asked with a smirk.

"I haven't heard from him directly," Adam said. "But I will hear from him one of these days."

"I hope so," Simon said. "Then we wouldn't have to hear you cry at night."

"I don't cry!" Adam said hotly.

"Benjamin said you did," Simon taunted. "He said you cried like a baby the first two nights you were here. I bet you cry all the time."

Adam roared and lunged out for the other boy. He swung as hard as he could for Simon's nose. The bigger boy was surprised by the quickness of Adam's hands. His fist made a sickening smack. Blood poured out of Simon's nose. In an instant, both boys were rolling on the ground, each trying to pound the other one into smithereens.

"Crybaby, coward!" Simon taunted. "You're just a chicken, face it!"

"Stop it!" Reuben pulled Adam off. Jude was holding back Simon, who was struggling with all his might to pull his arms free so he could go after Adam again.

"I'm not scared!" Adam yelled hoarsely, the tears streaming down his cheeks. "And I'm no coward!"

"Just stop it, both of you," Reuben said. "Simon, you know you weren't supposed to say anything about that."

"But you know that's what the crybaby did," Simon said shrilly. "I'm sick of this city-boy cousin acting so high and mighty all the time. I don't care if he is our relative. And I don't care if he could pick up Uncle Samuel's stupid stick."

"Dad said not to talk about it," Reuben said. "Now let's get back to work. Adam will pull the hay wagon until quitting time."

"Sure, the crybaby gets to do everything," Simon spat out. "Why would Uncle Samuel choose that sissy to do anything? It's just not fair that he should be Uncle Samuel's pet."

"But he's the only one who could pick up Uncle Samuel's staff," Benjamin said.

"Oh, shut up," Simon grunted. "Who cares what the crybaby does anyway?"

Adam wiped his eyes quickly. He didn't look at any of his cousins as he got onto the tractor. He was sure his face was still red. He felt hot and embarrassed and ashamed.

"They knew about me crying," he thought to himself. "They all knew all this time, but didn't say anything. I thought it was a secret."

Adam had looked forward to driving the tractor all day, but now the joy was gone. He started the tractor and put it in gear. At least he didn't have to face them sitting up on the tractor. He followed the long rows of hay bales down the field.

"No one tells me anything," Adam said to himself bitterly. "Of course they all knew. Benjamin is a big blabbermouth. And to top it off, they think I'm Uncle Samuel's pet. I didn't ask to be chosen for anything. It's just one more thing they'll hold against me."

He worried the rest of the afternoon. Part of the time he worried about what his cousins thought about him. The rest of the time he was worried about driving the tractor nice and straight. It wasn't as easy as it looked to drive in a straight line when the field was uneven and jerked the steering wheel back and forth. After an hour of holding on tight to the jerking steering wheel, Adam's arms were really aching. Still, he didn't want to let anyone know that it was harder than he had thought. He knew they would probably call him a weakling and all other sorts of names. He was glad that the day was over. He was especially glad that the hay wagon was full. The tractor would need to be driven back to the barn. Even though his arms hurt, Adam wanted the chance to drive on the open road where it was smooth and he could go faster.

"I get to drive the wagon to the barn, don't I?" Adam asked as they loaded on the last bale of hay.

"Why should he get to drive?" Simon asked. He rubbed his nose which was still red.

"The last person driving always gets to drive back to the barn," Adam said.

"The rules apply to family, our *immediate* family," Simon said. "You're just a cousin and a charity case at that. I don't know why Dad agreed to let you come here in the first place. I'll be glad when you leave with Uncle Samuel."

"None of you are doing me any favors," Adam spat out. "I hate being here. But I still should get to drive back to the barn. Don't I get to drive, Reuben?"

"I guess so," Reuben said. He looked at Simon and shrugged his shoulders.

"Good," Adam said. He turned the tractor toward the house.

"The City Boy might get lost," Simon taunted Adam.

"You're so funny," Adam patronized. "I can get back fine. Besides, I know about the shortcut."

"The one through the creek?" Reuben asked.

"Yeah," Adam said.

"It's still too soft," Reuben said. "You'll get stuck. Go by the road or you can't drive."

"Tell them you won't get stuck," a voice said suddenly next to him. Adam turned. Sitting on the side of the big rear wheel guard was that boy who looked just like Adam, and Adam could see right through him. The boy smiled and held up the box with shiny black sides. Adam looked at the box with sudden interest. Though it was a different size, he was sure it was the box with all the mysterious treasures.

"What are you doing here? Why did you bring the box?" Adam whispered.

"Who are you talking to?" Simon demanded.

"There's no one there," Benjamin added.

"Shut up," Adam hissed. He turned his back on his cousins and looked at the boy next to him. Then he looked at the box.

"Take the shortcut home," the boy said. "And don't let them ride on the wagon either. They just want to boss you around. They're just jealous that your great uncle likes you best. It's your turn to do things your way. Tell them to take a hike. When we get home, I'll let you look in the box. If you take the shortcut, you'll have plenty of time to see what's inside."

The ghost boy laughed and Adam smiled. Suddenly, what the boy said seemed to make perfect sense. "I won't get stuck," Adam said defiantly. "And you guys can take a hike."

Adam gunned the tractor and let out the clutch. The tractor jumped forward more quickly than he anticipated. He enjoyed being in control. He pushed the throttle forward so the tractor went faster. "I'll show those guys what a city boy can do. After all, Uncle Samuel did choose me over them."

He looked over at the wheel well, but the ghost boy was gone. "That guy comes and goes so fast," he said to himself. He wondered if he would be waiting at home with the box. That made him want to go even faster.

He looked back. Simon and some of the others were waving their arms at him, telling him to come back. He assumed they wanted to ride on the wagon since they had left their bikes at the house that day.

"Let them walk!" Adam shouted. "They deserve it after the way they've been treating me."

He pushed the throttle all the way forward. The tractor roared as he crossed over the dirt road that went the long way home. He looked back. His cousins began to run across the field after him as they saw him head for the creek. The tractor reached the creek bank sooner than Adam expected. He could tell by old tracks that he was in the place where they crossed. He slowed down and went down the bank of the creek.

"This is easy." He crossed over the thin trickle of water with the big tractor tires. As he approached the opposite bank Adam gunned the engine. He almost got to the top when the tractor seemed to stop moving, even though the engine was racing. He looked down. The big back wheels were spinning in the soft sandy dirt of the creek bank.

Adam pushed the throttle all the way forward. The big wheels spat dirt out into the air furiously. Then it all happened rather suddenly. The tractor began to lean and lurched forward. The front wheels left the ground as the tractor leaned even more to the side. The engine roared and Adam lost control of the tractor. Adam realized it was tipping over just in time to jump off.

He hit the sandy creek bank and rolled away as the heavy tractor slammed down on its side. The roaring engine sputtered and stopped.

The front wheels of the tractor spun in the air slowly as his cousins ran across the creek and over to where Adam lay.

"Are you all right?" Reuben asked.

"Look what you did!" Simon pointed to the tractor. The steering wheel was bent way to one side. The smoke stack was completely broken off. Gasoline was dripping out of a hose into the gray sand. The hay wagon was tipped over on its side. Bales of hay were all over the creek bed. A few had broken open, and loose hay was blowing in the slight breeze.

"You could have killed yourself!" Reuben looked both amazed and scared. "I told you not to come this way."

Adam nodded silently. It had happened so fast. His shoulder hurt where he had hit the ground. He looked and saw that the tractor was lying right on top of the place where he had been. He would have been crushed if he hadn't rolled away. Adam began to shiver at the thought.

"Wait till Dad sees this mess!" Benjamin said. "You broke our tractor."

"You're going to be in big trouble, City Boy," Simon said with a crooked smile. "You've really done it this time!"

Adam still shivered as he stared numbly at the mess he had caused. More than anything, he wished he could somehow turn back time and undo what had just been done. A sick dread filled his stomach. He had made mistakes in his life before, but this was serious. Why hadn't he listened to Reuben? Why had he even wanted to drive the tractor at all? Now no one would be driving the tractor. He wondered if he had broken it so badly that it couldn't be repaired. He began to feel even worse. No amount of wishing was going to undo this mistake.

"I was just trying to take a shortcut," Adam said softly. "I was just trying . . ." But he couldn't finish. His face was covered with tears by the time Simon and Benjamin began running toward the house to tell their father the news.

# GET AWAY

· · · · · · · ·

# 7

Adam wished he could disappear. Somewhere, somehow, there must be a hole, he thought, that he could just fall into and go away and never have to be in this place again. He already had gotten in trouble for stealing the tractor key. Adam dreaded to think what the punishment would be for ruining the tractor. He was sure he would have to clean the chicken house for the next fifty years, besides owing a ton of money for the tractor. What would Great Uncle Samuel think of such a mess? He would be especially disappointed.

Uncle Jacob roared up in the pickup truck. He glanced at the fallen tractor but walked directly to Adam. His face was filled with concern.

"Are you all right, son?" his uncle asked. "No broken bones?"

Adam shook his head. The tears that had finally stopped now started up all over again. He sobbed loudly. Uncle Jacob pulled him closer to his side. Adam shook as he cried. He buried his face in his uncle's overalls. He felt ashamed for the whole mess, and just as ashamed for crying about it, but he couldn't help it. There was no way he could stop. His uncle let him cry, and patted him on the back.

"You boys unload the hay and get the wagon back up on her wheels."

"What about him?" Simon demanded. "He caused this whole mess. Reuben told him not to come this way. But he and his city-boy ways wouldn't listen. He had to be a wise guy. Now he's nothing but a crybaby, just like always."

The words stung Adam like the lashes of a burning whip. The pain was too much to bear. He bolted from his uncle's side and ran down the creek bank. He ran up on the dirt road and headed toward the house.

"Hey, come back and help us, crybaby," Simon yelled.

But Adam kept running. He didn't look back. He shot down the road, running as if he were being chased by a monster out of his worst nightmare. He ran and ran until his sides hurt, but he didn't stop running. He ran up the driveway, but instead of going to the big farmhouse, he ducked inside the workshop near the barn. He flopped down in an old rocking chair that his uncle had recently fixed. He took deep gulps of air, trying to think.

"You really did it this time," a voice said behind him. Adam whirled around. The ghost boy sat in another chair, smiling his thin crooked smile. "Everyone will hate you for sure. You need to get out and get out quick."

"What do you mean?" Adam asked.

"What do you think, stupid?" the boy asked. "Run away. Get the train in town and get out of here. You have enough money. You can buy a ticket. But you won't have any money left once you pay for that tractor.

It will cost a zillion dollars to fix that stupid mistake. You better get out while the getting is good. Everyone hates you now. And Great Uncle Samuel will really be disappointed, especially after he made such a big deal about choosing you."

What the ghost boy said seemed to make sense. Everyone must hate him by now. He would get his money, go to town, get a train ticket and get away.

Adam jumped out of the chair and ran out of the workshop. His aunt was in the yard hanging out sheets and towels on the clothesline. Being careful so she wouldn't see him, he went around to the back of the big farmhouse. He went in the kitchen door and ran upstairs to the room he shared with Benjamin. He opened his duffel bag at the foot of the bed. He kept his money in a wallet hidden in a coffee can. He stuffed the wallet in his back pocket. He quickly put about half his clothes into the duffel bag and left the rest. He didn't want to carry any more weight than was necessary.

He got up to leave and paused. He felt guilty for wanting to run away. He wondered if he was making a mistake.

"You aren't making any mistake." Adam knew who it was without looking. The ghost boy was sitting on the dresser. "Use your beads. They'll give you strength."

Almost automatically, Adam touched the beads hanging around his neck. Without thinking he rubbed the golden paint off one bead, the last one on the string. He looked down at it sadly. Inside the dark sphere he could see the broken tractor and the mess of hay. Simon was pointing his finger at him and saying, "He's nothing but a crybaby."

"See how much they hate you?" the ghost boy taunted. "You better get out of here quick before they get home. Those boys will beat you up for sure when their dad isn't looking."

"I won't let them hurt me again," Adam muttered out loud.

"You'll need more money. You better take extra," the ghost boy said. "Benjamin has plenty. He won't need it."

Adam paused. Having more money would probably help, especially in an emergency. He walked over to the closet. He reached up and got an old cigar box off the top shelf. The box had several dollars in bills and coins, and two chocolate candy bars, one half eaten.

"So that's where he keeps his chocolate," Adam said with surprise. Chocolate bars were rationed, like a lot of other things since the war began. Adam usually ate any candy he had right away. But Benjamin saved his candy and just ate a little at a time to make it last. Adam counted the money and took about half the bills. He put them in his pocket. As soon as he did, he felt guilty.

"It's not really stealing," the ghost boy said, sitting on the bed watching him. "You can pay him back when you get settled with your sister and aunt. It's just an emergency loan. You better get some chocolate for your trip too. You have to eat."

Adam took the uneaten chocolate bar, closed the cigar box and put it back on the shelf. Even though he felt the dull nagging feelings of guilt, he pushed them out of his mind. He had a long trip ahead of him, and he felt anxious to get going.

He picked up the duffel bag and quickly walked downstairs. He made sure the back door didn't slam as he left. His aunt was still hanging up clothes.

He ran to the barn. Adam saw his bicycle back in the corner behind a stack of hay bales. An old red Spirit Flyer bike covered in dust leaned against the wall.

"You don't need that stupid bike," the ghost boy said. "Go on foot."

"I can get to town faster on a bicycle," Adam said. "You can fly on these things, you know."

Adam hopped on the bike. As soon as he sat down on the dusty seat, he heard the sound of a blowing horn. "What is that?" Adam asked. He cocked his head. Then he realized in horror that the sound was coming from the horn on his bike, steady and loud. "Ssshhhhh. Be quiet, you stupid bike."

Adam slapped the horn with his hand, but the horn kept blowing. Adam looked all around. He decided to pedal and just get away. The big balloon tires rolled a few feet but then stopped. Adam stood up on the pedals, pushing with all his might, but the tires refused to turn. The blowing horn only got louder.

"The horn is loud enough to be heard in the next county," the ghost boy said. "Leave the bike and get out of here while you still can. That bike isn't going anywhere."

"Stupid bike," Adam got off it. "Why don't you help me when I need you?"

He kicked the big tires in disgust. The blowing horn got even louder. Adam picked up his duffel bag and ran out the back door of the barn. Outside, he could still hear the horn. He ran through the yard, carefully climbed over the white picket fence and headed out through the garden. He ducked through a barbed wire fence and ran into the corn field. He looked over his shoulder as he ran between the stalks of corn. No one was following.

At the end of the corn field he hit Glory Road, which led into Centerville. He listened carefully. If the horn was still blowing, he couldn't hear it. The road was deserted. He decided to pace himself by running and walking. The town of Centerville was almost eight miles away and the duffel bag was heavy.

Adam walked and ran for more than an hour. The sun dropped lower in the sky. He imagined that his cousins would be getting ready for supper soon. The thought of food reminded him that he was hungry.

"I should have made a sandwich or something before I left," he thought to himself. Adam took out the candy bar. He ate two bites and put it back in his pocket. He started running again. The duffel bag felt heavier than ever. He wished he had left more of his things back at the house. As he rounded a curve in the road, he saw a farmer fixing a flat tire on his pickup truck. The man in faded blue overalls and a big straw hat was lowering the rear bumper with the jack as Adam walked up.

"Need a ride into Centerville?" the farmer asked in a friendly manner. Adam had seen the man before at the feed store, but he didn't know his name.

"I'd love a ride."

The man looked at Adam's duffel bag and raised an eyebrow. He put the flat tire and jack in the back of the pickup.

"Going on a trip?" the man asked.

"Out to see my sister. She lives with my aunt. My aunt works in an airplane factory."

"Lots of work in those airplane factories these days," the farmer nodded. "Put your bag in the back and let's go."

Adam tossed the duffel bag in the back of the pickup and climbed in the cab.

"I hope I can convince the ration board to give me a new inner tube," the man said as they rode toward town. "I've got patches on my patches on the one that just went flat. I'll sure be glad when all this rationing business is over."

"The sooner the better," Adam agreed.

They rode in silence. The man drove around the Centerville town square and parked in front of the hardware store.

"Thanks for the ride." Adam hopped out. He got his duffel bag and began walking. He cut across the center of the square in front of the big courthouse.

He walked a few blocks west and south to the train station. Three cars and one pickup truck were parked in front of the red brick building. An old horse rail and cement water trough were near the doorway into the station. He wondered if anyone ever rode horses into town. He knew of several farmers who still used a team of horses or mules to plow and work the fields.

He walked inside to the ticket counter. No one was behind the small window. He saw a stack of train schedules on the counter. He picked one up and sat down on a long wooden bench. A few other people were sitting on other benches, waiting.

He had just started to read the schedule when he heard a train whistle. Everyone in the building walked outside. Adam looked at the schedule. The columns of times and numbers were hard to understand. He took the schedule and his duffel bag and walked outside on the platform.

A large black locomotive rolled slowly into the station. The big wheels clanked and the brake lines hissed as the hulking machine finally stopped. A conductor stepped down and placed a little stool in front of the door on the passenger car. Three women got off with two little boys. The conductor helped the women with their bags. Adam followed him inside the station, wanting to ask a question about the schedule.

But once inside, the conductor disappeared into the office. Adam walked over to the window, but he still couldn't see anyone. He sighed, then went back to the bench and sat down by his duffel bag.

"Hey, come outside," a voice said. Adam looked up. The ghost boy was outside on the platform near the train. He was holding a dark box. Adam was sure it must be the mysterious box he had seen the day before. He picked up his bag and walked out of the station. The ghost boy ran off the platform to the rear of the train. Adam was curious and hurried after him.

The ghost boy ran past the passenger cars and the freight cars. When he got to the rear of the train, he disappeared around the red caboose. Adam ran to catch up. He crossed the tracks carefully.

When he got to the other side, he was going to say something to the ghost boy. But the ghost boy was gone. Instead, he saw another boy bent down, looking underneath the train. He stood up and wiped the dirt off his hands. He was taller than Adam. His clothes were dirty. A dusty carpet bag was at his feet. His red hair was greasy. Adam guessed he was fourteen or fifteen years old.

"It's only you," the boy said with relief. "I saw legs, and I thought it might be the conductor or the guy in the caboose. We better get on before they see us."

"Get on?" Adam asked. "You mean get on the train?"

"Sure," the boy said. "You came back here to hop a ride, didn't you?"

"I was going to buy a ticket. But I couldn't find the conductor."

"You've got money for a ticket?" the boy asked with interest.

"I think so," Adam said slowly. He didn't like the way the boy was staring at him. "I never really got a chance to ask. I'm heading out to Seattle, Washington, to see my sister."

"Traveling alone?"

"Yeah," Adam said simply.

"Seattle's a long way from here." The boy looked at Adam carefully. "You better save your money. I can show you how to go for free. I'll show you how to get all the way to Seattle without spending a single dime."

"Really?" Adam asked.

"Sure. I've gone all over the country and all I use is my wits. Right now I'm heading downstate to catch up with a carnival. I work there. They feed you good and give you a place to sleep. You ought to try it for a while. You can make lots of money if you know the angles."

"Really?"

"Tons of money," the boy said confidently. "Stick with me, and I can teach you how to live by your wits."

"You know how to sneak rides on the train, like a hobo?" Adam asked.

"Why pay when you can ride for free?" the boy asked with a sly smile. "The scenery's the same. The boxcars ain't too bad if you get one with hay or something soft to sleep on. But we got to get on fast, or someone will see us and kick us off. They can be tough on you if they catch you."

The boy with red hair ran up the tracks. He climbed up a small metal ladder on a rusty red boxcar. He threw his bag through the big open door and climbed inside the car.

Adam felt scared and excited at the same time. When he saw the ghost boy pop his head out of the same boxcar, Adam decided to give it a try. He climbed up the little ladder and pushed his duffel bag through the door. He jumped inside just as the train shuddered and clanked and began to move.

The boxcar seemed huge inside. Adam didn't see the ghost boy, but the other boy was sitting on his carpet bag, leaning against the wall. Adam dragged his duffel bag over and sat down. He looked around, wondering where the invisible boy had gone.

"He's here one second and gone the next," Adam thought, feeling peeved about it. "I'll never get a hold of that box, even though he said I could have it."

He leaned against the wall. The whistle blew loudly as the steel wheels rolled faster. Adam took a deep breath and looked out the big door. The town of Centerville was soon left behind. The whistle blew again as the train headed into the falling night.

# TRAIN RIDE

· · · · · · · ·

# 8

The train picked up speed. Adam moved farther away from the big sliding door of the boxcar. "Shouldn't we close that door?" Adam asked anxiously.

"Are you kidding?" the older boy asked as if Adam was stupid. "You don't want it to lock on us. I've heard of some guys getting drunk and locked up in these cars and dying 'cause they couldn't get out. They starved to death."

"Really?" Adam asked. He looked at the big door fearfully.

"Don't worry," the boy said with a knowing smile. "You won't fall out. At least not unless you're really stupid."

"I'll watch it." Adam inched farther away from the big door.

"My name is Dudley." The boy with greasy red hair smiled. "Got any food on you?"

"No," Adam said sadly. "Just part of a candy bar."

"Made with chocolate?"

"Yeah."

"Let's have some, I'm starved," Dudley said eagerly.

Adam hesitated. He had wanted to save the candy. He had planned to eat on the train, in the dining car. But that was for passengers who had paid for a ticket.

"Come on," Dudley said. "It's the rule of the rails that you share what food you got with your friends."

"But I only have half a bar left."

"That's better than nothing. I haven't had any chocolate in days."

Adam reluctantly took out the rest of Benjamin's candy bar. He carefully broke it in half. Dudley grabbed a half without waiting to be asked. He stuffed the whole thing in his mouth and chewed. He smiled, tasting the sweet chocolate. "Someday I'm going to own a candy store," he said greedily. "I'll have all the candy bars I want. I'll eat ten a day if I want. I'll eat ten just for breakfast."

"You can't do that if they're rationed."

"But if you owned the store, they'd belong to you, and you could eat whatever you wanted," Dudley insisted. "I know because I met up with some rich kid whose parents owned a store. He told me they snuck candy all the time. They didn't ration anything."

Adam didn't know what to say. The inside of the boxcar had gotten very dark in a short time. The sky was cloudy and there was no moon or stars to bring any light.

"It's really dark tonight," Dudley said softly. "We might as well sleep. This train will stop in Lewistown early tomorrow morning. The schedule says it will be there for several hours. We can get off there, and I'll show you the carnival."

"It's in Lewistown?" Adam asked.

"Sure. It's part of the county fair. Carnivals follow a schedule, just like the trains. They go from county to county, as part of the fairs. They're good places to work. You should try it."

"I really love carnivals and fairs," Adam said eagerly. "I like going on the rides. One time, before the war, my friends and I got to go to the fair for my birthday. We rode every ride three times, including the big roller coaster. We got to play at all the game booths. I won five glass plates and three mugs for my mom at the penny toss. And I won a huge stuffed bear at the shooting gallery. I gave it to my sister Thelma. It was a great day."

"If you work at the carnival, you get to go on the rides for free."

"For free? All you want?"

"All you want," the boy repeated. "Of course, you have to do it on your time off. You got to work too. You should come work with us. It's good money."

"I don't know." Adam thought about riding all the rides he wanted. "I guess I would try it if I wasn't going to Seattle."

"I'm going to get some sleep," Dudley said. "See you in the morning."

"Yeah." Adam tried not to think about how hungry he felt. Eating only a small piece of the candy bar seemed to make him more hungry, not less.

The boxcar got darker and more lonely by the minute. Adam leaned back on the duffel bag. He thought about being at the farm. He used to lie on the bed in Benjamin's room and feel lonely and homesick. But at least he was in a real bed in a real house with people he knew, Adam thought. The night seemed much closer and more vast as he looked out the big boxcar door. He figured his aunt and uncle would really be worried by now. Great Uncle Samuel would probably be upset too.

"Why did I get on this stupid train?" Adam thought to himself. "Why did I run away? If only I hadn't tipped over the tractor trying to take a shortcut. Reuben and Simon knew that it was dangerous. They could have stopped me if they really wanted to. I bet they wanted me to crash so they could gloat and not let me drive the tractor anymore. But it's too late now. I had to get out of there. They all hate me. I can't go back."

Adam looked down and realized he was rubbing one of the dark beads. He hadn't even realized it was in his hands. He turned it over and around in his fingers, bitterly wishing things had turned out differently.

"Mom and Dad shouldn't have made me go to Uncle Jacob's in the first place. It's all their fault," Adam thought. He rubbed the bead harder. "And if those stupid Nazis hadn't started the war, Mom and Dad wouldn't be over there and in danger all the time. How come no one stopped the Nazis a long time ago? Why isn't this stupid war over yet?"

Adam wasn't sure who to blame, so he blamed whoever came to mind. The list grew longer and longer as the train rolled along. After a while, the sound of the steel wheels and the rocking motion of the train began to feel familiar. The night was chilly. Adam got a long-sleeved shirt from his duffel bag and put it on over his other shirt. He was lost in his chilly bitter thoughts when Dudley interrupted the dark silence.

"What was that?" Dudley asked. He sat right up. He pointed in the direction of the big open boxcar door.

"What was it?" Adam asked fearfully.

"I don't know," Dudley said slowly. "I thought I saw something out there. It was right outside the door. For a moment I thought it was a bicycle. I must be seeing things."

"A what?"

"I know it sounds crazy," Dudley said seriously. "But I saw something that looked just like a bicycle wheel. It had spokes and everything."

Adam leaned forward to look out in the darkness. Something was out there. He saw it, but only for an instant. A glint of light from a distant farmhouse reflected off a piece of chrome. He thought he saw a large bicycle moving along in the shadows beside the train. Adam rubbed his eyes. If it was a bicycle, he was sure it had to be a Spirit Flyer bicycle since it was six feet off the ground. He stared into the darkness, but either it was gone or had become invisible.

"I wonder if that's my . . ." Adam said slowly.

"Wonder what?" Dudley asked.

"Nothing," Adam said. "It couldn't be. We must be seeing things. I'm going to try to get some rest."

"Good idea," Dudley said in the darkness.

Adam drifted off into an uneasy sleep, but not Dudley. The older boy waited, staring out the boxcar door into the night. After an hour, the clouds cleared and the moon began to shine. Dudley listened to Adam breathing heavily in sleep.

"You awake, farm boy?" Dudley asked softly.

As if to answer, Adam snored slightly and turned on his side. His back pocket with his wallet was in view of the moonlight. Dudley stared hungrily at the tip of the wallet, wedged between Adam and the boxcar floor.

"Now it's time to relieve my little friend of his fat wallet," Dudley said to himself. The older boy crawled over by Adam. He slid his hand slowly across the boxcar floor. His fingers just touched the leather of the wallet when it happened. A large object moved out of the shadows in the boxcar. A big balloon bicycle tire rolled over Dudley's creeping hand and pinned it to the boxcar floor.

"Aaaaaaacckkk!" Dudley screeched in fear. He yanked and pulled back. "Let me go! Let me go!!!"

Adam woke up from the noise. In the moonlight, he saw a strange sight. Dudley was on the far side of the boxcar. His eyes were wide with fear and he was pointing at something. That's when Adam saw the old red Spirit Flyer bike standing on its tires next to him. He blinked in surprise. Somehow he knew that it was his Spirit Flyer. He was almost as surprised as Dudley to see the bike in the back of a train car.

"What is that thing?" Dudley demanded.

"It's a bicycle." Adam was still groggy from sleep.

"I can see it's a bicycle, but how did it get here?"

"I don't know," Adam said truthfully. "It's my bicycle, and I guess it found me."

"Found you?" Dudley asked, his voice still quivering. "Don't let it hurt me."

"Why would it hurt you?" Adam asked. He yawned. He was too tired to think about the old bicycle. For some reason, he didn't feel as lonely as before. He felt tired and almost peaceful. "Let's talk about it in the morning. I want to get some sleep."

"Yeah, let's sleep." Dudley scooted far away from Adam and the odd red bicycle. Adam laid his head back down on his duffel bag and closed his eyes. In the moonlight, Dudley continued to stare at the bicycle with wide eyes.

"I'll get that fat wallet yet," Dudley said softly. "Just you wait." He watched the boy and bike until the night and rolling train finally rocked him to sleep.

# OFF THE
# PATH

· · · · · · · ·

# 9

Adam woke up the next morning feeling stiff. The train was not moving. The morning sun was shining through the big boxcar door. Adam rubbed his eyes. In the night he had dreamed his Spirit Flyer bicycle had flown into the boxcar and stayed beside him.

"What a crazy dream," he murmured as he stretched his arms. Then he saw the big balloon tire off to his left. The red Spirit Flyer was leaning against the boxcar wall. Adam stared at the old bicycle, not sure what to think.

Dudley yawned and woke up. When he saw the big red bicycle, his eyes opened wide and he jumped back, very much awake. "I thought it was just a nightmare," Dudley stammered. "I dreamed about a horrible red bicycle that chased me all over the place. It looked exactly like that bike."

"It's just my Spirit Flyer," Adam said.

"I think it must be haunted. How could a bicycle get here? This train didn't stop at any stations."

"I'm not really sure how they work," Adam said honestly. "They are unusual bikes."

"You don't have to tell me. I'm getting out of here."

Dudley looked uneasily at the big bike and then hopped out the wide boxcar door. Adam walked over to the door. The boxcar had stopped over a crossroads. A winding dirt road led out through a field toward the back entrance of the Lewistown fairground about a quarter of a mile away. Adam smiled when he saw a huge ferris wheel sticking up into the sky.

"That's the carnival I was telling you about," Dudley said. "Like I told you, a clever kid can make lots of money working there."

"I don't know. I'm headed for Seattle."

"Suit yourself." Dudley looked at Adam's wallet. He licked his lips. "I bet a smart kid like you could win a lot of prizes at the game booths. And since you know me, I can get you a ride on the ferris wheel for free."

"Really?" Adam asked. He looked at the ferris wheel and other rides in the distance. A lot of fun seemed to be just waiting for him.

"Think about it." Dudley looked at Adam's wallet once more. But something else caught his eye. The old red bicycle began to roll all by itself toward the boxcar door. Dudley stared at the bike in horror. In a flash, he turned and began running down the dirt road to the carnival.

"What's the matter with him?" Adam wondered as he watched the boy running away. The big front wheel of the rolling bike bumped into the back of Adam's leg. He turned around, surprised to see the bike. The bicycle backed up a foot and rolled forward again, hitting his leg.

"What are you doing?" Adam asked out loud. He immediately felt silly for talking to a bicycle. The old bicycle rolled back and then came forward again, hitting his leg a third time.

"Ok, ok." Somehow Adam knew what he was supposed to do. He lifted his leg over the middle bar and sat down on the worn seat. The old bicycle immediately turned in a circle inside the empty boxcar until it was aimed at the wall. Adam gripped the handlebars, more than a little scared. Maybe Dudley was right in thinking that the old bike was haunted.

The old headlight flashed on by itself. Adam gasped. The light shone so brightly on the rear wall of the boxcar that Adam had to squint. When he finally opened his eyes again, he saw a surprising sight.

He saw the creek bed on Uncle Jacob's farm. He saw himself driving the tractor and hay wagon up the bank. He watched in horrified fascination as the tractor began to tip. Adam cringed, seeing the awful scene unfold. The big tractor tipped farther to one side as the big back wheels dug into the sandy bank. As he watched, he saw something deeper. He saw a man in shining white clothes appear at the side of the tractor as it began to fall over. Adam saw himself jump away. As he hit the ground, he saw the man in white hold the big tractor up so it wouldn't fall on top of Adam. The mysterious stranger only held it for a few seconds, but it was long enough for Adam to roll out of the way.

"Wow," Adam whispered. The man in white clothes stepped aside and bowed as another man arrived. Adam recognized this man. The Prince of Kings walked past the tractor and right out of the creek bank into the rays of light coming from the Spirit Flyer. He walked straight toward Adam, who was still sitting on the bicycle in the boxcar.

"Whoa!" Adam yelped, trying to back up. But the big balloon tires on the bicycle didn't move. The Prince of Kings walked through the light and stopped right in front of Adam. The scene of the creek bank and tractor disappeared as the light on the old bicycle turned off. The Prince didn't look angry, like Adam expected, but he didn't look exactly happy either. More than anything, he seemed concerned, the same way his Uncle Jacob had looked when he had arrived at the scene of the tractor accident. The Prince stared quietly at Adam, who shifted uneasily on the seat.

"You are off the path," the Prince said in voice that sounded like water running in a deep river.

"Off the path?" Adam asked in a small squeaky voice. "You mean I drove the tractor off the path and caused it to crash? I know now it was a mistake to take that shortcut home."

"You are off the path," the Prince repeated.

"Off the path?" Adam repeated. As much as he tried to resist the thought, he knew deep inside what the Prince meant. He looked down at the floor, feeling ashamed. He could feel the Prince watching and waiting. Adam took a deep breath. Still looking down at the floor, he spoke. "You mean because I ran away? So what am I supposed to do now?"

"Get back on the path where you got off."

"You mean go back to Uncle Jacob's farm?" Adam protested. "But I can't go back. They all hate me."

"You took things that didn't belong to you," the Prince said solemnly.

"You mean Benjamin's money and candy bar?" Adam asked. His face turned red. He didn't think anyone had seen him. "I'm just borrowing those things," Adam hotly insisted. "I didn't really steal them. I'm going to pay him back when I get to Seattle."

The Prince didn't say anything. But he didn't have to. Adam avoided his gaze by looking down. "You are off the path," the Prince said. "Return to where you left the path. Return what was stolen. You reap what you sow. If you walk in the light, you will find life and the freedom of your deepest wishes. But if you go off the path, you will stumble in all kinds of darkness."

"But I'll be in big, colossal trouble if I go back," Adam mumbled. "You don't understand. They're already mad at me. Now they'll be extra mad since I ran away."

"Let your Spirit Flyer take you back to the path," the Prince said in a kind voice. "I will walk with you through your shame."

Adam's whole body was tense, struggling to decide. The thought of going back and admitting he had stolen the money and candy from Benjamin seemed much worse than wrecking the tractor. At least the tractor wreck had been an accident of sorts. He wished he could say the same about taking Benjamin's belongings.

"At least get something to eat so you can decide on a full stomach," a whining voice said behind him. Adam knew without looking that it was the ghost boy.

"Can't I get something to eat first?" Adam asked. "I don't feel so good. I haven't eaten since yesterday's lunch."

Immediately, the old red bicycle began to move. It stopped by his duffel bag, which he picked up and tied on the back. Then the boy and bicycle rolled out the wide door of the boxcar into the morning sunlight. Adam got a better grip as the bicycle flew along the side of the train and crossed the tracks. The Spirit Flyer glided down into the parking lot of the Lewistown train station. Right in front of him, across the street, Adam saw Frank and Rosie's Cafe.

He could already smell the pancakes and bacon as he pedaled over to the cafe. He parked the bike by the front door and went inside. Adam ate two stacks of pancakes with lots of syrup, and several sausages. He drank three glasses of cold milk before he finally felt full and ready for the day. He paid for the food and went outside.

The ghost boy was waiting, sitting on the front bumper of a car. He smiled when he saw Adam. "Feeling better?" the ghost boy asked.

"Sure."

"Then let's go over to the carnival," the ghost boy said.

"But the Prince said I should go back to Uncle Jacob's farm."

"Yeah, but he didn't say you had to go back right this minute, did he?" the ghost boy asked.

"Well, not exactly," Adam said with a frown. "But I think that's what he meant."

"He just said to go back sometime, right?" The ghostly figure smiled. "Besides, he isn't here now. You might as well go to the fairgrounds now, because if you go back, you'll be cleaning the chicken house the day the family goes to the fair, remember?"

"I guess you're right," Adam said slowly.

"You bet I'm right," the ghost boy replied. "Have fun now while you've got the chance. You deserve it."

"I should have some fun before I go back to that prison." Adam nodded his head bitterly. He rubbed an invisible bead that hung around his neck. He hopped on the Spirit Flyer.

As soon as he got on, the bicycle began to roll across the parking lot. The boy and bicycle crossed the street and rode beyond the train station. Adam could see the fairgrounds in the distance. The big ferris wheel was turning. Adam smiled. As the front wheel left the ground, the bicycle turned away from the fairgrounds and headed north toward Centerville.

"Hey!" Adam said as the Spirit Flyer glided up into the air. "You're going the wrong way!"

The bicycle quickly soared up into the sky. Adam knew the Spirit Flyer was taking him back to his uncle's farm.

"Not yet!" Adam yelled as the bicycle shot up toward the clouds. He jerked the handlebars back in the direction of the fairgrounds. The old red bike turned slowly in the sky. As it turned, it seemed to lose power and began to wobble and shake.

"What's wrong with you?" Adam asked in exasperation. "I'm the rider here. I just want to look for a while."

Adam jerked the handlebars and headed straight for the fairgrounds. He began pedaling to hurry the bike along. But the pedals turned slowly and pushing on them was hard. The carnival looked better and better by the second. All the rides were turning and the grounds were filled with people busy having fun. Something looked familiar. Then he saw it. A large banner in front of the ferris wheel and other rides said *Fattooka's Fantastic Midway*.

"It's the same carnival that I saw when I was back in the tree!" Adam said in surprise. The boy forgot about the Prince's words. He just wanted to get closer. He pushed down on the pedals harder, trying to go faster so he could get a better look. For a moment, he thought he could hear someone speaking to him. He felt a vague nagging sense of something being wrong. Then he could hear the Prince's words clearly. "Return to where you left the path."

"I'll go back," Adam said out loud. "I just want to see the fair before I do. Besides, this is the same one I saw when I was in the tree, isn't it? I thought I was supposed to come here."

Even though he could still hear the warning of the Prince, Adam kept pedaling toward the big ferris wheel. He passed over the fairground fence and headed toward several long buildings that housed farm animals for exhibits. The bicycle wobbled more than before.

"I'll just stay for an hour," the boy said. "That can't be a problem, can it?"

As if to answer, the red bicycle abruptly stopped in the sky. The pedals stopped turning as the horn began to blow.

"Come on, you stupid bike," Adam demanded. He groaned as he tried to push the frozen pedals. The horn blew louder. The louder it blew, the more the boy resisted.

Then it happened. The horn quit blowing and the bicycle began to fall. Adam pulled on the handlebars desperately, but the Spirit Flyer continued to drop. Adam yelled as the bicycle fell through the sky like a giant stone.

# ON THE MIDWAY

· · · · · · · ·

## 10

The old red bike zigzagged toward the earth. Adam yelled even louder. The boy and bike sailed over a wooden fence behind one of the exhibit barns and crashed into a big wet mud hole inside a corral. The soft mud stopped the bike, but the boy kept going. He flew over the handlebars and made a somersault, landing on his bottom with a big wet splat. A large pig squealed as it jumped back.

"Hey kid, get out of that pen!" a voice yelled. "What do you think you're doing? You can't ride a bicycle in there. That old boar will chew you up if you don't get out." Adam hopped up. A tall farmer with two children was glaring at him from outside the gate. The mud smelled terrible. The whole back of his pants was coated with the sticky mess. Adam turned around. His Spirit Flyer was lying sideways in the mud. The duffel bag was still carefully tied on the back.

"Nice piggie," Adam said fearfully as he picked up the bicycle. "At least my duffel bag didn't get too dirty." He carefully rolled the old bike away from the hog toward the gate. His feet slipped and slid and he almost fell twice. The farmer opened the gate as Adam pushed the bike through. The two children crinkled their noses in disgust when they smelled the mud on Adam's pants.

"You're lucky that old hog didn't take a bite out of your leg," the farmer said. "And what in tarnation are you doing with a bicycle in a pigpen?"

"Just an accident," Adam mumbled. He looked down at his pants and groaned. The smell was terrible.

"There's a hose at the back of the stock shed over by that row of trucks," the farmer said. "Go clean that stink off you, boy."

The man pointed toward a long shed. Adam nodded and began pushing the mud-caked bicycle. He tried to ignore the people staring at him. He knew his face was turning red.

"Stupid bike," Adam muttered. He rounded the corner of the shed and was relieved to find a pipe with a handle and a hose attached. He quickly pulled up the handle. Water spurted out of the black hose. He turned it on his pants and rubbed them under the water until all the sticky mud was gone.

By the time he was finished with the hose, his pants were soaking wet and water was in his shoes. He sighed in disgust, and turned the hose on the Spirit Flyer. After another five minutes, the bicycle was mostly clean and dripping wet. Adam turned off the water and shook his hands so they would dry. He still felt foolish from being in the pigpen. He glared at the old bicycle.

"I don't know why I got stuck with a dumb bike like you," Adam spat out. "I didn't ask you to follow me. Why don't you just leave me alone?"

Adam was about to insult the bike even more when he smelled the scent of cotton candy floating through the air. He could hear the music from the carousel and the sound of children laughing. For the first time in a long time, Adam remembered that it was summer, a time when children were supposed to have fun.

"You just got here." The ghost boy leaned against the shed wall. "Take a look around. Have some fun. Don't worry about that crazy bicycle."

"I should have some fun after that dumb bike tricked me, falling like that." The boy checked his back pocket. His wallet was wet but still there. Once again he could hear faint words telling him to get back on the path. But the words weren't as loud this time, and Adam was still mad about landing in the pigpen.

"I'll stay here as long as I like," he announced to whoever might be listening. He quickly pushed his Spirit Flyer into the stock shed. Most of the stalls had sheep and goats staring out from behind the gates. But the one on the end was empty, except for a few hay bales. Adam pushed his bike inside and leaned it against the wall. He opened the duffel bag. He took out dry, clean clothes and quickly changed. He stuffed the wet clothes into the duffel bag and then hid it behind a hay bale. He left the stall, making sure the gate was shut tightly.

"I'll come back when I'm good and ready," the boy said to the bike. He turned and walked toward the midway. Adam didn't notice the boy with the red hair and red shirt watching him leave. Dudley smiled, looking at Adam's wallet.

Adam walked directly toward the rides. He crossed under the banner that said *Fattooka's Fantastic Midway*. People were everywhere, crowded around the sideshows, game booths and rides. Children carried balloons, stuffed animals and dolls that they had won at the game booths. Some were eating cotton candy or caramel apples. Above the noise of the rides, he heard the music of the merry-go-round. Men and women called out as Adam passed by their booths.

"Step right up and be a winner. Prizes, prizes and more prizes! All it takes is five cents and a good aim. Step right up, hurry, hurry, hurry. Be the next big winner at the Ring Toss!"

Adam walked around the whole midway, trying to decide on a strategy. He checked his wallet. He had plenty of money. He rode the carousel first. Then he went on a small but scary roller coaster called the Mighty Mite. After that, he rode each ride once, intending to save the ferris wheel for last. He walked by it several times, hoping to see Dudley so he could get a free ride. An old man and woman ran the ferris wheel. The boy with red hair wasn't to be seen.

After riding the rides, Adam tried his luck at the game booths. He played at the ring toss, pitched nickels at dishes, manipulated the little cranes in the glass booths, shot at moving ducks and bottles at the shooting gallery, threw baseballs at metal milk bottles. Adam was surprised how many kids his age and even younger were working at the booths and rides. He remembered what Dudley said about the carnival being a good place for kids to work.

Adam visited every game booth in the midway, but he didn't win even one time. He kicked at the dirt as he walked away from the shooting gallery.

"What lousy luck," Adam mumbled. "I wonder if these games are rigged so you lose. I'm not that bad of a shot. I've always won at the shooting gallery before."

Adam checked his money. He still had plenty left. Looking at all the bills, he felt guilty for a moment, remembering that some of the money really belonged to Benjamin. Adam quickly stuffed the wallet back in his pocket, not wanting to think about it. Even so, for a moment he could see the Prince's face looking at him, telling him about stumbling in darkness.

In the center of the midway, near the ferris wheel, smoke drifted upward above a long trailer with lots of windows. Adam sniffed the air, smelling the hamburgers and french fries and hot dogs. It was near noon, and long lines of people were waiting to place their orders. Since rationing had started, being able to buy a hamburger without a ration coupon was a real treat for most folks, and they wanted to take advantage of the opportunity.

Adam smelled the rich aroma and walked closer. A sign above the trailer said *Fattooka's Famous Foods, Herod Fattooka—Proprietor.* A large, fat man with greasy black hair and a greasy black mustache was flipping hamburgers at the grill inside. He wore a dirty white apron over his black pants and shirt. He looked up and barked out an order toward a young girl with blond hair who hurriedly carried a metal tray filled with food to the counter. He yelled again and a boy brought the man a pan full of uncooked hamburgers and hot dogs. Adam stood in line until it was his turn at the counter. He waited for the big man to take his order.

"Mary, get those fries out, quick," the man yelled. "Quit being such a slowpoke girl."

"Yes, Mr. Fattooka." The girl hurried over to a big machine and lifted a basket of steaming hot french fries and dumped them into a big tub. She jumped back so the steam wouldn't burn her.

"Faster, you lazy girl!" Mr. Fattooka yelled, and with one quick motion, he struck the girl with the flat side of his spatula so hard that she yelped and jumped. Then he shoved her hard. Adam blinked in surprise. The girl said nothing, but Adam could see tears welling up in her eyes.

"You shouldn't do that!" Adam exclaimed to the big fat man. He looked up from his grill and frowned at Adam.

"Mind your own business, kid," the big man snapped, rubbing his lips with the back of his hairy arm. "Do you want to buy something or not?"

"I'm not sure," Adam said.

"Then get out of the way, farm boy," the man said. "Next!"

Adam moved over as some kids behind him pressed up to the counter to order. The fat man glared at him once more. Adam looked at the girl with blond hair. She smiled at him shyly. Adam smiled back. She was pretty, but seemed awfully thin and tired. So did the other boy who worked behind the counter.

Adam decided the food could wait. He put his wallet back in his pocket. He didn't want to face the big fat man again so soon. He walked by a row of booths. He stopped in front of a colorful mural advertising *Fattooka's Freaks and Fabulous Wonders of the World*. Large garish pictures covered the mural: a big snake with two heads, a woman with a beard, a tall skinny man that looked like a skeleton, a tremendously fat man and fat lady, shrunken heads on poles, and a mummy in a golden coffin. But the most ugly and frightening was a picture of a wild man in a cage gnawing on a bloody bone.

A dwarf stood on the ticket stand, yelling through a megaphone at the people as they walked by. "Step right up. See Rose and Randy, the couple that weighs a ton! See Lily the Lion Lady. Hear her roar, touch her mane! See the shrunken heads from South America. See Sarx the Wild Man from the jungles of Borneo. Raised among cannibals half his life. Don't get too close to his cage. He still longs to eat his favorite food, a diet of human flesh!"

Adam kept walking past the exhibits. He wished he'd ordered some food. He walked over to the ferris wheel. He saw a boy with a red shirt and bright red hair taking money.

"Now I can get a free ride!" Adam said to himself.

He walked over. An older man controlled the machinery that made the ferris wheel go around while Dudley collected the money.

"One dime, one dime for a ride on the big wheel," Dudley shouted. "One thin dime."

"That's kind of expensive," Adam said. "Maybe I should ride for free."

"That's cheap, kid," the boy snarled, turning to see who had spoken. When he saw Adam, Dudley grinned crookedly.

"So you decided to stop by after all?" the older boy said.

"Do I get to ride for free?" Adam asked.

"Sure." Dudley turned to the older man. "This is the friend I told you I met on the train." The older man smiled. He was missing several teeth and the ones he did have were almost black.

"Any friend of Dudley gets a complimentary ride, courtesy of Mr. Herod Fattooka, Proprietor." The old man laughed. "Just stand in line with the others and wait your turn."

Adam joined the line of children who had already paid. The ferris wheel kept spinning. Dudley collected the money from the others and had them stand in line. Finally the big wheel slowed to a halt. Dudley lifted the bar on each bucket and let the old riders get out and the new riders get in. When it was finally Adam's turn, he bumped into Adam from behind, shoving him into the seat of a blue bucket.

"Hey, quit being so rough!" Adam complained. "You don't have to push me."

"Shut up and enjoy the ride," Dudley whined. "I hope you ain't afraid of heights." He laughed and clicked the safety bar into place. The bucket jerked up into the air, swaying back and forth. Adam looked down. The way the metal bucket rocked and swayed made Adam feel uneasy. He rubbed his finger over the blue chipped paint. The ferris wheel seemed ancient. He felt even more uneasy as the big ferris wheel lifted him up bit by bit as the other buckets were emptied and filled.

Under the roar of the machinery he heard a loud heavy clanking noise as the wheel turned. He craned his head to see if he could locate the source of the noise. With a jerk and a thump, the big wheel started spinning around and around. Each time they came down close to the ground, the car Adam was riding in jerked and shuddered. Large greasy gears and a thick heavy chain turned the big ferris wheel. Adam stared at the large turning gear. Something looked out of place. Then he noticed that one of the teeth on the gear was broken off part way. Adam shifted in his seat. He looked the other way trying to just enjoy the ride and not worry about it.

At the highest point on the ferris wheel, he got a great view of the midway. It reminded him of being on his Spirit Flyer. Everyone screamed and laughed as the big wheel went around and around. Thinking of his Spirit Flyer made Adam feel uneasy. Once again he could hear the voice of the Prince telling him to return to Centerville, to get back on the path.

"I'll just finish this ride, get a hamburger and get out of here," Adam said uneasily. "That can't do any harm. I'll buy a train ticket home and be there by this evening."

The big ferris wheel spun around several times and then began to slow down. Bucket by bucket, Dudley let the old riders out and the new riders on. He didn't say anything as Adam got out.

Adam felt hungrier than ever. He walked back to the food trailer. He waited in line five minutes, then stepped up to the counter.

"What you want, kid?" Mr. Fattooka asked in hurry.

"A hamburger, french fries and a soda," Adam said.

"Coming up," the man said. "That's forty-five cents."

Adam reached for his wallet to get out a dollar bill. But his wallet wasn't there.

"My wallet!" Adam yelled. He twisted around and looked in his back pocket in disbelief. "I've lost my wallet! That had all the money I'd saved!"

Adam frantically checked all his pockets. His face felt hot and his heart was beating hard. He checked his pockets again, but the wallet was definitely gone.

# STOLEN TWICE

· · · · · · · · ·

# 11

You don't got no money, kid?" Mr. Fattooka asked with a frown.

"I can't find my wallet," Adam moaned. "I had it a few minutes ago when I was here. Maybe I left it on the ferris wheel."

"No money, no food," the big man said. "Next!"

Adam moved to one side. He looked on the ground. Then he looked at the ferris wheel. He quickly ran through the booths and rides over to the big wheel.

"My wallet, I lost my wallet," Adam said breathlessly to Dudley. The boy stared at Adam and shrugged his shoulders.

"We ain't responsible for things getting lost." Dudley grinned. "Are we Frank?"

"It ain't our problem, kid," the old man said.

"But can't you ask people as they get off the ferris wheel if they saw it?" Adam asked. "I was in one of the blue buckets."

"You can ask 'em," Dudley said. "I've got work to do."

Adam watched and waited till the big wheel began unloading. He asked every passenger in a blue bucket about his wallet. None of them had seen it. The ferris wheel started spinning again.

"It ain't here, kid," Dudley said. "Too bad. Maybe someone turned it in up at the food shack. That's where they keep the lost and found. Ask Mr. Fattooka. He might know, but I wouldn't count on it."

Adam felt like crying. He ran back to the food shack. He waited in line again to talk to the big man behind the grill.

"I lost my wallet and the boy at the ferris wheel said you have the lost and found here," Adam said. "Has anyone turned in a brown leather wallet with black stitching on it?"

"Anyone turn in a lost wallet, Mary?" the big man asked the girl. She looked at Adam and then Mr. Fattooka. She shook her head.

"No wallets, kid," the big man said without interest.

"Are you sure?" Adam asked.

"I'm sure," Mr. Fattooka said, as if very bored. "You want to order something?"

"No." Adam walked away from the counter. The frying foods smelled better than ever. Adam felt a stab of hunger in his stomach.

"I just better get out of here," Adam muttered to himself. He walked back through the midway despondently. He shuffled through the animal exhibits, through the Future Farmers of America barn and over to the shed with the goats and sheep. He went to the rear entrance. He opened the gate to the rear stall.

The Spirit Flyer bicycle was gone! He looked behind the pile of hay. His duffel bag was gone too. Adam ran outside to make sure he was at the right building. He saw the water faucet and black hose where he had cleaned himself up earlier. He was sure it was the right building.

"My bicycle and duffel bag," Adam moaned. He ran through the building, looking in each stall. All he saw were sheep and goats. He asked a boy brushing a goat at the far end of the building if he had seen anyone with an old red bicycle.

"Let me think," the kid said. "Wait a minute. Seems like I did see a kid with a red shirt and red hair looking around down there a few minutes ago. He carried something over to all those parked trucks. It might have been a duffel bag. I didn't see any bicycle."

The boy pointed at the long row of carnival trucks parked near the fairground fence. Adam ran over. The big trucks and trailers all had padlocks on the back doors. Adam ran past each truck and looked between them. He didn't see Dudley or his duffel bag or his bike. He ran back to the boy brushing the goat.

"Was this guy wearing black pants?" Adam asked.

"Maybe," the kid said. "He was bigger than you."

"About fourteen or fifteen years old?"

"Yeah, probably," the kid said.

"You think you would recognize him if you saw him again?" Adam asked.

"Probably."

"Can you come with me?" Adam asked. "I think I know who this guy might be."

"I can only go for a little while. I have to get my goats ready to show."

"Follow me." Adam walked quickly through the rows of buildings and corrals back into Fattooka's Fantastic Midway. But when they got to the ferris wheel, an older woman was taking the money, not Dudley.

"Where's Dudley?" Adam asked the older woman. She had stringy gray hair and was missing two of her front teeth.

"He ain't here," the woman said.

"But I saw him earlier," Adam insisted.

"He might be working another ride," the old man named Frank said. "He could be anywhere. Check the food shack."

"Do you have time to stop by the food shack?" Adam asked.

"Barely," the boy said. "Let's hurry."

They ran to the food shack. Mr. Fattooka, Mary and the thin boy were the only ones at the food shack.

"Where can he be?" Adam asked.

"I've got to be going," the boy said. "I'll be here tonight, though, for the evening show."

"I can't wait around that long, I've got to be somewhere myself." But as soon as he spoke, Adam realized that he wouldn't be going anywhere without his Spirit Flyer or money for a train ticket. "Maybe I will be here. Thanks for trying to help me."

Adam wandered aimlessly through the midway, trying to think. He looked, but he didn't see the red-haired boy anywhere. Even though there were hundreds of happy, excited people all around him, Adam felt terribly alone. He felt like crying but knew that wouldn't do any good. He stopped by the House of Crazy Mirrors and stared at himself in the mirror by the ticket taker. In the mirror, he looked short and fat.

"I should have never stopped here," Adam said sadly. "The Prince told me to return. How could I be so stupid?"

"You *are* stupid," a voice said. Adam looked more closely at the mirror. Suddenly his distorted image split into two Adams. The other Adam was a little shorter, but had a familiar grin. "You really are a moron. You couldn't follow directions on how to tie your shoes. Your uncle is going to be mighty disappointed. No one will trust you to do anything ever again. Why they picked you in the first place is a mystery to me."

"Leave me alone," Adam said.

"You *are* alone," the ghost boy answered. "That's why I came to keep you company. You can't go back now. You're stuck here."

"Shut up." Adam walked rapidly away from the mirror. His feet plodded along. He sniffed the air and smelled the delicious hamburgers. He walked back to the food shack and stood near the counter. He watched the big fat man turning the hamburgers and hot dogs. The big man looked carefully at Adam. After he flipped all the burgers, he walked to the counter.

"Hey, kid, come here," the fat man said. Adam walked over. "You want to eat a good meal? A burger, lots of fries and a cold soft drink?"

"I'd love to eat, but I lost all my money," Adam said hopelessly. "I haven't eaten since breakfast."

"I'll give you a meal if you go to work for me this afternoon," the fat man said. "I need someone to peel potatoes. I lost a boy in the last town. If you come to work for me, I'll give you supper. If you work till quitting time, I'll throw in a dollar."

"I don't know," Adam said. He thought for a moment. If he waited, maybe he could find Dudley. Adam took a deep breath.

"Is it a deal?" Mr. Fattooka asked.

"Ok," Adam said reluctantly.

"Good," the big man said. "I'm Mr. Herod Fattooka. I own this midway. Come around to the side and get an apron and a knife. Mary can show you where to peel the potatoes."

Adam walked in the side door of the food trailer. Mr. Fattooka talked to the girl. When she saw him, she smiled.

"Thanks for sticking up for me earlier," she said softly.

"That's ok," Adam said.

"Let me show you the potatoes," Mary said. They walked to the back of the trailer. In a small room filled with canned goods, Mary showed Adam a big tub, a bucket with water and a big fifty-pound sack of potatoes.

"I've never seen so many potatoes," Adam said in amazement.

"There's lots more," Mary said. She picked up a potato and quickly began peeling it with a small knife. After it was peeled, she dipped it in the bucket of water and dropped it in the tub.

"You're fast."

"You'll get the hang of it after a while," Mary said with a smile. "I better get back. Mr. Fattooka has a bad temper."

"Why do you work for him?"

"I don't have anywhere else to go," the girl said sadly. "I never had a dad, and my mom ran off with some salesman last May leaving me and my brother, Danny. We didn't have any relatives back in Halleysburg. When the carnival came through, my brother caused an accident and broke something that belonged to Mr. Fattooka. He threatened to call the police if we didn't go to work for him and pay off the debt. He said the police would make Danny live in a reform school and I would be sent to an orphans' home."

"You mean you have to work for him?" Adam asked.

"Yeah, or we'll be in trouble. We owe him over fifty dollars still. Danny and I want to stick together. We just got each other. It's not so bad. Lots of kids work for Mr. Fattooka doing different things. He gives us a place to sleep and food to eat. I better go now."

Adam nodded. He wanted to ask about Dudley, but that could wait. He sat down and attacked the big sack of potatoes. He peeled them slowly at first but gathered speed. He stood up to stretch every once in a while. Time passed, but the bag seemed to empty slowly. Mr. Fattooka came back twice and took the peeled potatoes. He frowned at Adam and said nothing.

When the sack was halfway done, Mary came back with a little paper bag of french fries and a bottle of catsup.

"Mr. Fattooka said you could eat these," she said.

"Thanks," Adam said. Even though his appetite for potatoes had dropped, the fries still tasted good since he was so hungry. "I wish he'd send a burger."

"We never eat until after the supper rush is over," she said. "You're new. You'll have to do potatoes a few days or so until you can get a better job, like working in one of the booths."

"I'm not sticking around here," Adam said defiantly, stuffing the fries in his mouth. He chewed them quickly. "I'm supposed to go on an important journey, but I got sidetracked, unfortunately."

"Sidetracked?" the girl asked.

Adam told her about his parents being overseas and about running away from the farm. The girl listened intently, and seemed more and more interested the more Adam talked. He told her about riding on the train and meeting up with Dudley.

"So I'm waiting to see if I can find Dudley again," Adam said. "I think he may be the one who took my duffel bag."

"He may have taken it," the girl said angrily. "Up north, a couple of towns ago, Dudley disappeared. He just showed up again today. I heard he got arrested and sent to reform school for being a thief. Maybe he escaped."

"Reform school?" Adam asked. "I wondered why he was on the train."

"Mr. Fattooka was acting real secretive about it," Mary whispered. "I've heard that some of the kids, including Dudley, are pickpockets. They work around the rides and booths taking whatever they can sneak. They steal stuff when people are distracted, like getting on or off rides, or playing at the game booths. My friend Jane said they give most of the money to Mr. Fattooka. He's the greediest man I ever saw. All he wants is money. He and Dudley get together and talk each night. Dudley doesn't live with the rest of us kids in our trailer. He stays in the nice trailer with Mr. Fattooka and Frank and Olive."

"The old couple at the ferris wheel?" Adam asked.

"That's them," she said. "They're related to Dudley somehow. And I heard they're cousins or something of Mr. Fattooka. They used to run the carousel, but now Mr. Fattooka put them in charge of the ferris wheel, ever since he got in trouble a few towns back."

"What kind of trouble?" Adam asked.

"The ferris wheel almost broke. The police came and told him to shut it down. They said it was unsafe. Mr. Fattooka said he'd fix it. But he

# *102*

couldn't find the right new part because they don't make 'em since the war started. He shut it down for the rest of that week, but when we moved, he started it going again. I don't think it's safe, but he doesn't care. The ferris wheel makes the most money of all the rides except maybe the carousel."

"I wondered if it was safe when I was riding in it," Adam said. "I heard odd noises and felt some bumps."

"I wouldn't ride in that old scrap heap if you paid me cash money." Mary suddenly got quiet. "Don't tell anyone what I told you. Especially about Dudley. He'd beat on me. He's meaner than a snake."

"I won't tell," Adam replied softly. "But where is he? I would like to ask him some questions about my bike and duffel bag. Maybe he and his pickpocket friends know something about my wallet too."

"He'll be around tonight," Mary said. "But you better watch out. I've seen him beat up lots of kids. He likes picking fights with kids smaller than him."

"But he can't get away with stealing stuff," Adam protested.

"Just be careful. I've got to go."

Adam nodded. He sat down on the tiny stool and began peeling potatoes again. As he sat, he planned ways of confronting Dudley. "I'll get to the bottom of this," Adam vowed angrily under his breath.

He finished peeling the big sack of potatoes by suppertime. Mr. Fattooka hauled in another whole bag. Adam groaned. His fingers were cramped and sore from peeling.

"When can I eat?" Adam asked.

"In an hour," the big man said. "You keep working. You get that bag done and I'll throw in an extra two bits."

"Sure," Adam said. He peeled for an hour. Mary brought a plate of food. Adam ate it quickly, gulping down the soda.

Mary smiled as she watched him eat. "You'll feel better after you eat. That's what my mama always told us before she ran off."

"You don't know where she is?"

"Nope. We should be able to pay off Mr. Fattooka by the end of the summer. Then we'll go back to Halleysburg and see if Mama's come back."

"What will you do if she doesn't return?" Adam asked.

"I don't know," Mary said simply. "I better get back before Mr. Fattooka starts yelling."

Mary left. Adam looked at the sack of potatoes with a frown. He picked up the knife and began peeling again. The task seemed endless. By midnight, he could hardly move his fingers, they were so sore. But Adam wasn't thinking about his fingers. He was thinking about his lost money. Not only was his money gone, but the money he had taken from Benjamin was gone too.

"Yep, the stolen money got stolen twice," a voice said behind him. Adam whirled around. The ghostly boy sat on a counter near the pots and pans. He seemed bigger and taller than before.

"Shut up," Adam said angrily. "I was just borrowing Benjamin's money. I was going to pay him back."

"Sure you were," the ghost boy said. "But it's too late now, isn't it?"

Just then, a stocky little man walked into the back room. Adam blinked his tired eyes. He recognized the man who took the tickets at the freak show.

"I'm locking up for the night," the dwarf said brusquely. "Let's go."

Adam followed the little man outside. He looked around hoping to see Dudley, but the midway was all but deserted. The rides were quiet and dark. "Where's Mr. Fattooka?" Adam asked. "He's supposed to pay me."

"He's gone to bed," the dwarf said. "You'll have to talk to him in the morning."

"In the morning!" Adam protested. "But he owes me a dollar and a quarter."

"It ain't my problem, kid." The little man turned and walked away, disappearing among the dark rides.

Adam felt tired and discouraged and totally alone. The midway seemed eerie and spooky at night. He walked past the closed tented booths and exhibits. He wasn't sure where to go. He wandered out to the animal barns. He stopped at the pigpen where he had crashed that morning. The same big boar was there, grunting contentedly in the mud.

"I should have gone back when I had the chance," Adam said softly.

The goat and sheep barn was still open. Adam went to the stall were he had left his duffel bag and the Spirit Flyer, hoping against hope he might find either one. But the stall was empty. He was dead tired. His hands ached and his eyes seemed full of sand. He sat down on the straw and leaned back against a hay bale. He closed his eyes to think.

Adam heard soft, beautiful music. He opened his eyes a crack. The music got louder and Adam saw a huge golden, glittering hallway opening out in front of him. Beyond the hall was an even more magnificent room. Adam opened his eyes wider and sat up straight. Half his body was still in the stall, but the other half of him was resting in the beautiful room in front of him.

"Rest, my child," a voice said. Adam knew the sound of the voice because he had been hearing it on and off all day: this was the deep clear voice of the Prince of Kings. The voice seemed to vibrate right through him. When the sound finally left, Adam rubbed his eyes and looked deeper. The beautiful palace room shimmered before him and slowly faded. The merest outline of the golden walls remained as if they were made of the soft notes of music.

"Maybe I'm dreaming," Adam said. Yet he felt sure he was awake. He was puzzled, but he was too tired to try to figure it out. He suddenly felt very safe. The beautiful music flowed like a pleasant creek. A lamb bleated softly in the darkness. So much had happened that day. He yawned once, stretched out on the floor of straw and fell fast asleep.

# THE CRYSTAL BALL

• • • • • • • •

# 12

Adam woke up the next morning with straw tickling his nose. He opened his eyes slowly. For a moment, he saw the huge golden room in front of him. The place was beautiful and peaceful. Adam felt totally at rest.

"How did I get to this place?" the boy wondered. He had dreamed all night long about playing in a magnificent palace. The place was fantastic. When you jumped, you could go a hundred feet high. And when you imagined things, they just appeared the way you pictured them. He had thought of a field of enormously tall flowers and they appeared. He wanted to fly over the flowers and instantly he was soaring above them in the bluest of blue skies.

A loud bleating goat in the next stall made Adam open his eyes wide. He looked down and saw a golden shining key in his hand. The key was attached to a tiny golden chain that hung around his neck. He let go of the key and rubbed his eyes. The magnificent palace slowly disappeared. Adam shook his head. It took him a moment to remember he was at the fairgrounds in Lewistown and he had slept in the sheep and goat barn.

"What a dream," Adam murmured and yawned. "It seemed so real."

He stood up and stretched. Inside the barn, farmers were busy feeding their sheep and goats. A growl in Adam's stomach reminded him of his own hunger. Adam reached for his wallet. When his hand felt the empty pocket, Adam suddenly remembered what all had happened. Being in the palace in his dream had almost made him forget his troubles. Unconsciously, he reached for the dark beads around his neck.

"I'm out of money," Adam lamented, touching the empty pocket again. A familiar fear settled over the boy. He looked down and saw the huge chain of beads around his neck. The golden key was also hanging over his heart, but this time he reached for the dark beads, now as big as golf balls.

"Mr. Fattooka owes me a dollar and twenty-five cents," the boy murmured. "At least I can get that and eat."

Adam turned to open the gate, but a large red Spirit Flyer bicycle blocked his path. "My bike!"

"Forget the bike." The ghost boy, who was now at least a foot taller than Adam, stood outside the gate. "Get your money from Fattooka and see if you can find your wallet. Dudley might be around, and he'll know something."

"You're right." Adam pushed the bike, trying to move it out of the way. The stubborn wheels seemed to barely turn. The tires skidded across the straw and dirt. "Come on! I've got to get what's owed to me at least."

Suddenly the bike rolled easily. Adam shoved it over to the side wall and smiled triumphantly. "I'll be back in a few minutes after I get what they owe me."

Adam walked past the animal barns and exhibits back into the midway. None of the rides or booths were open since it was so early. But smoke was coming out of the food shack. As Adam got closer, he saw the whole place was full of carnival people eating breakfast.

Mr. Fattooka was by the grill, cooking mountains of pancakes, bacon and sausage. Mary and her brother Danny carried trays of food over to the tables of waiting children and adults.

"Mr. Fattooka," Adam said. "I came to get the money you owe me."

The big man turned around. He frowned when he saw Adam. He picked up a sausage off the grill with his fingers, put the whole thing in his mouth and chewed it up slowly. He wiped his mouth with the back of his hairy arm.

"You said you'd give me a dollar and quarter if I worked until quitting time, remember?" Adam said.

"Did I?" the big man asked.

"Yes," Adam said firmly. "So I'd like to get my money now."

"You don't like working for Fattooka?" he asked as if his feelings were hurt.

"It's not that. It's just that I've got to be going."

"I see." The big man rubbed his chin. "I'll tell you what. I've got a little job for you to do. You do that, and I'll give you breakfast for free and your money."

"Sure," Adam said eagerly.

Mr. Fattooka walked over to a table and talked to the dwarf and a lady with long black hair. They followed the big man back to the counter.

"I want you and Stump to help Esmerelda move some of her things," Mr. Fattooka said. "When you're done, come back and Fattooka will give you a good breakfast."

"Ok," Adam said. Esmerelda smiled at him. The Gypsy lady wore a purple turban and a purple dress. She had the longest fingernails Adam had ever seen. They were painted blood red.

"Come on, kid," Stump the dwarf said. Adam followed them outside through the midway to Fattooka's Fabulous Freaks and Wonders of the World Exhibit.

They walked inside, past the two-headed-snake cage, past the shrunken heads and the mummy. They passed through a narrow hallway into another small room with a row of bars across the front of the cage that held Sarx the Wild Man. Sarx had his back turned. He was noisily eating something from a tray. His wild, uncombed black hair stuck out in all directions. Several large bones lay on the floor of the cage.

"Was he really raised among the cannibals?" Adam whispered to Stump the dwarf.

"Of course he was," the dwarf said seriously. "I don't go near that cage." To prove his point, he stayed on the far side of the hall in front of the cage. Adam moved over to the far side of the hallway like the dwarf.

They stopped in the hallway before the next room in front of a small closet. Esmerelda unlocked the big padlock on the door.

"I always keep my crystal ball and table locked up each night," Esmerelda said. "You two will carry it to my booth outside."

Stump went in the closet. He picked up one end of a small wooden table. In the center of the table was a shiny glass ball on a small pedestal. Adam stared at the crystal ball curiously. Esmerelda saw him and smiled.

"Welcome to the future, young man," Esmerelda said in low husky voice. "I can see you have a deep interest in what's going to happen in your life. I read palms. I read tea leaves. I read the crystal ball. I can tell you many secrets. Tell me, my boy, what do you read to know the future?"

"The only thing I ever read that told about the future was *The Book of the Kings*, I guess," Adam said honestly.

"I never read that book!" the woman growled. She turned and spat on the floor. "I can contact the spirits of the dead."

"Why would you want to do that?" Adam asked. "I think I'd rather talk to someone still alive."

"This boy is an idiot," the woman said with disgust. She seemed strangely upset. "Just help Stump move my table. I'm afraid you are in for some bad luck, my boy."

Esmerelda walked out ahead of them, still muttering and complaining in a language Adam didn't understand. Adam picked up his end of the table and began backing down the hallway. He backed in front of the cage that held Sarx the Wild Man. There was barely enough room for the table. Since Adam had to hold the center of the table, he felt uncomfortably close to the bars of the man's cage.

"Hurry up," Esmerelda hollered. "Don't be such a slowpoke."

Just as Adam was about to walk backward faster, he saw something move in the cage. Adam turned just as the dirty hand of Sarx shot through the bars.

"Yeaoooooowww!" Sarx howled as he lunged.

"Aaaaaccccckkkkk!" Adam screamed, dropping the table and jumping back all in one motion. The crystal ball wobbled, then fell off the table. It hit the floor and shattered into a thousand tiny pieces of glass.

"My crystal! My crystal!" screamed Esmerelda. She slapped her forehead as if she would faint and ran from the room, wailing and crying.

"Look what you did, you stupid idiot," Stump said. "You're in big trouble now, boy."

"But I didn't mean to break it." Adam looked down at the glass hopelessly. A large piece quivered and rocked on the floor. From the broken shape of it, he realized that the crystal ball had been hollow on the inside, like a Christmas tree ornament.

"You really did it now, kid," Stump said. "I wouldn't want to be in your shoes."

"But you saw how that guy jumped at me," Adam protested.

"What's going on here?" roared Mr. Fattooka as he stormed into the room. He looked at the broken glass on the floor, then glared at Adam. "You broke Esmerelda's crystal ball."

"It was an accident," Adam said. "Sarx scared me. I couldn't help it."

"You'll pay for this mess," Mr. Fattooka said. "What do they cost, Esmerelda?"

"One hundred dollars," the Gypsy woman said. Tears filled her dark eyes as she pounded her chest with her fist. "My crystal, my crystal. This boy breaks my heart. This boy must pay me what he owes."

"But I haven't got a hundred dollars," Adam said hotly. "I don't even have a dime."

"Then your parents must pay," Mr. Fattooka said.

"But they aren't here," Adam said. "They're in England helping fight the war."

"Then *you* must pay," Mr. Fattooka said firmly. "Pay me what you owe, or I will turn you over to the police. They know what to do with clumsy boys like you."

"Don't take me to the police," Adam pleaded. "It was all just an accident. Ask Stump. Sarx came at me like a crazy man. He stuck his arm through the bars at me."

"You shouldn't have gotten so close to the cage," Mr. Fattooka said. "The signs state that he is a beast and a wild man."

"But I was carrying the table, and there was nowhere else to go," Adam replied, his voice cracking.

"You tripped on your stupid clumsy feet." Mr. Fattooka grabbed Adam by the collar with one hand. With the other hand he slapped Adam in the back of the head. "Quit making excuses, you lazy boy. You are only trying to cheat Fattooka and Esmerelda."

"But I'm not trying to cheat anyone." Adam jerked out of the big man's grasp. He looked at the thousands of pieces of broken glass. He could feel tears begin coming to his eyes.

"I knew this boy was bad luck," the Gypsy woman snorted. "I saw it in the crystal just before he dropped it."

"But it was an accident," Adam repeated weakly.

The big man grabbed the boy by the collar again. He lifted Adam up off the ground so the man and boy were face to face.

"Nobody cheats Fattooka," the big man hissed. Adam was so close he could smell the sour odor of the fat man's breath. His yellow teeth clenched down in anger. "You will pay me what you owe."

"But I don't have any money, I told you," Adam said feebly.

"Then you will work for Fattooka until you pay off your debt," the greasy man said. "One dollar a day is a hundred days."

"That's over three months," Adam said desperately. "I can't stay here three months."

"Then I will give you to the police, and you will stay in reform school longer than that," Mr. Fattooka hissed. "So what's it going to be? You work for me, or I give you to the police?"

Adam hesitated, trying to think. The big man pushed his face so close that his nose almost touched Adam's forehead. He shook Adam until the boy's teeth chattered.

"I take you to the police," the big man said in disgust. He yanked Adam by the collar so hard that his shirt ripped. Adam slipped, almost falling on the pieces of broken glass. Mr. Fattooka slapped him on the back of the head again and began dragging him toward the door.

"I'll work for you. I'll work for you," Adam blurted out. "Please don't take me to the police."

"That's better," Mr. Fattooka grunted. He leaned down again, his face just inches away from Adam's. "But remember. You must pay me everything, or I will give you to the police. If you try to run away, I will send my boys after you. They will catch you. They are rough boys. They hurt boys who try to cheat Fattooka, do you hear me?"

"Yes," Adam said, his voice cracking.

In the cage, Sarx the Wild Man howled and beat on his chest. He ran to the bars and lunged toward Adam. Even though he was out of reach,

Adam jumped back so hard that he hit the opposite wall, hurting his shoulder.

Stump came into the room carrying a broom and dustpan. Without a word, he handed them to Adam.

"You clean the mess you made and then come to the food shack," Mr. Fattooka said. "You will eat breakfast and then work for me today."

"Ok," Adam said.

"You say, 'Yes, sir,' to Fattooka," the man instructed.

"Yes, sir, Mr. Fattooka," Adam said quickly. He looked down at his feet. He began sweeping the floor, staying as far away as possible from Sarx the Wild Man. Mr. Fattooka, Stump the dwarf and Esmerelda all left together, talking in a foreign language. Adam didn't understand a word.

The boy gripped the broom tighter. Tears began to fill his eyes once more. His shoulders shook as he sobbed. Nothing was turning out the way he had planned. As Adam swept, his future seemed as shattered as broken pieces of glass spread across the floor.

# PAYING
# MR. FATTOOKA
· · · · · · · ·

# 13

**After he cleaned** up the glass, Adam went outside. Mr. Fattooka was waiting. He followed the big man back into the food shack. He tried to wipe his watery eyes so Mary and her brother Danny wouldn't see, but he wasn't quick enough. When he saw her watching, he looked down at his feet.

"Eat quick!" Mr. Fattooka ordered. "And don't discuss our business with anyone. I don't pay some kids as much as you, so just keep quiet about what happened with the crystal ball and how you plan to pay off your debt. You understand me?"

Adam nodded and sat down at the long table where all the other boys and girls were eating. Over twenty boys and girls were rapidly finishing off their breakfast. Mary stayed at the grill helping Mr. Fattooka make pancakes and sausage.

Adam quickly piled his plate high with pancakes and sausages. As he ate, he looked over at the table of adults. Dudley was sitting with the older people. But what was more unusual was all the others at the table. There was a very tall, skinny man picking at his food. Next to him were two of the biggest, fattest people Adam had ever seen. A woman with a large mane of hair and hair on her face was next to the others. Stump the dwarf was at the end of the table, laughing and talking.

"Better eat fast." Danny sat down next to Adam. "We're late. When Mr. Fattooka says breakfast is over, it's over whether you're finished or not."

"I believe you." Adam tried to eat faster. He wanted to tell Danny about the accident, but then he remembered Mr. Fattooka's warning. As he ate, he couldn't help but look at the assortment of odd characters at the next table. Danny saw him looking.

"It's just the freaks." Danny talked as he chewed. "You get used to them. They're all pretty nice, except Stump. He's almost as mean as Mr. Fattooka. He's the reason we got stuck in this place. He caused the accident."

"What happened?" Adam asked.

"Well, I was helping Stump when—"

"Clear the plates, Danny," Mr. Fattooka shouted. "Everyone get to work. Now!"

Danny got up quickly and began picking up plates. Everyone got up immediately and started outside. Adam still had most of his food left on his plate. He began eating faster. Mr. Fattooka scowled at him. The big man walked over.

"Breakfast is over," Mr. Fattooka said.

"I was just trying to finish up the—"

Adam suddenly found himself flying through the air. He hit the ground hard on his bottom. Mr. Fattooka lifted his foot as if he was going to kick him again.

"Fattooka said breakfast is over," he growled. He pointed a fat finger at Adam. "You come with me."

Adam nodded and got up quickly. He followed the big man outside. Mr. Fattooka walked through the midway to the animal barns and sheds. When they reached the sheep and goat barn they stopped. Mr. Fattooka talked quietly to a man in blue overalls for a few minutes. Then the two men shook hands. Mr. Fattooka picked up a scoop shovel leaning against the wall. He carried it over to Adam.

"Your job today is to clean the barns," Mr. Fattooka said.

"Clean the barns?" Adam asked. "All of them?"

"Of course."

"But that could take days!"

"Of course," the fat man said. "We are here for the rest of the week. The local people ask me to supply a boy and I do. I will subtract it from what you owe me. One dollar a day."

"But the barns smell terrible," Adam protested. "They're as bad as my uncle's chicken house. And they're bigger!"

"You work for Fattooka now, boy," the big man said gruffly. "You do as I tell you and don't argue or you will regret it." He raised his large hairy arm, as if he was about to slap Adam. The boy ducked back.

"Ok," Adam said flatly. He took the shovel.

"Mr. Green will tell you where to work," Mr. Fattooka said. "Mary will bring you lunch at one o'clock or so, if we aren't too busy."

"Yes, sir," Adam muttered.

The man in the blue overalls had Adam start in the shed with all the pigs. Adam felt like he would gag because the smell was so strong. "You do one stall at a time," the man in blue overalls said. "Carry out the old floor in the wheelbarrow. Push it up that wooden ramp at the far end of the fairgrounds over there. Dump it off the end of the ramp into the pit below."

"Why is that ramp so high off the ground?" Adam asked.

"Because there's lots to haul, and it keeps the pile smaller in circumference and inside the pit area," the man replied. "After the end of the week we'll load it all up on a truck and haul it out."

"Ok," Adam thought. The end of the ramp looked dangerously high.

"When you get the stall empty and clean, bring in fresh sawdust and straw from behind that barn over yonder." The man pointed to a distant barn.

Adam nodded wearily. He slid the big scoop shovel into the stinky mess and began filling the wheelbarrow. When the wheelbarrow was full, he pushed it outside over to the wooden ramp at the edge of the fairgrounds. The ramp was forty feet long and fifteen feet off the ground where it stopped at the peak. With considerable effort, Adam pushed the wheelbarrow up the ramp to the edge and tipped it forward. The muck fell onto a small pile in the pit below. The cement pit was shaped like a large U. Adam turned the wheelbarrow around and headed back to the stall.

As he went back inside the pig barn, the boy was unaware that he was being observed from a distance. Mr. Fattooka and Dudley stood by a long blue trailer, watching him work.

"I still get my money for finding him and bringing him in, don't I?" Dudley asked the big fat man.

"Of course you get your money," Mr. Fattooka said. "Don't you trust Fattooka?"

"Well, I never got paid for the kid back in Youngstown," Dudley said.

"But he didn't even stay the night," the fat man said. "He ran off."

"But I brought him in."

"They have to stay on a few days to really count," Mr. Fattooka said. "It's like fishing. I don't pay for fish that get away. I pay when the fish is landed."

"You mean 'sucker,' " Dudley said and laughed. Mr. Fattooka took out his wallet. He took two bills and gave them to the redheaded boy. Dudley smiled as he pocketed the money.

"You think you can get him to work the midway with the other boys?" the hairy man asked.

"Sure he will," Dudley replied. "Once he gets tired of shoveling manure all day, he'll be glad to join us. He'd have to be a real idiot to keep doing that." Dudley laughed and the large man smiled. Together they turned and walked toward the crowded midway.

Adam worked steadily for several hours. The stink was terrible, but after a while he got more used to it. By noon, he had finished half the stalls. He stood up to stretch when he noticed a boy with red hair watching him. Dudley smiled when he saw he had been discovered.

"You got one of the best jobs in the fair," Dudley said with a smile. "How's it going?"

"It stinks, that's how it's going," Adam replied angrily. "I don't know how I got stuck here, but I don't plan to do this the rest of my life."

"I wouldn't let Mr. Fattooka hear you say that," Dudley sneered. "I knew a boy who tried to cheat him once. That was a big mistake."

"I shouldn't even have to be here," Adam said. "Where have you been, anyway? I was looking for you yesterday. Someone said they saw you yesterday snooping around the sheep and goat shed where my duffel bag got stolen."

"What do you mean?" Dudley asked defensively. "You think I stole your bag? Is that what you're saying? I didn't steal your bag. I put it in the trailer where all the kids stay because I knew it would be safer there."

"Are you sure?" Adam asked.

To prove his point, Dudley ran over to a blue trailer. He unlocked the door, went inside and returned with Adam's duffel bag. He carried it over to Adam.

"See?" Dudley said.

"Why didn't you tell me? And how come you put it in the trailer to begin with?"

"Because I figured you'd be working here," Dudley said with a smile. "And see, I was right."

Adam wasn't sure what to say. The whole story seemed fishy somehow.

"It will be waiting for you on an empty bunk tonight." Dudley ran back over to the trailer, put the duffel bag inside and returned to talk. "I heard you broke a valuable piece of property." Dudley grinned. "You shouldn't be so careless."

"It wasn't my fault that I tripped and broke that stupid crystal ball. That crazy Sarx jumped at me and scared me. Now Mr. Fattooka says I have to work for him or else. But he can't force people to work for him, can he?"

"I wouldn't ask too many questions, if I were you," Dudley said. "You don't want to get on the wrong side of Mr. Fattooka. I've seen him throw lots of kids in jail. They're probably still rotting there. Besides, you can get better work than this."

"What do you mean?"

"I mean there are other ways to pay off your debts a lot faster than you will by shoveling that manure."

"Quicker than a dollar a day?" Adam asked. He looked at Dudley curiously. "I think I'd rather do anything than be stuck out here all day."

"I don't blame you. A smart kid can earn a lot of money around here if he knows the angles," Dudley said. "You could probably pay off Fattooka in a couple of weeks."

"Really?"

"Sure," Dudley said. "Maybe in a week if you're lucky and know how to hustle. A smart kid can find money just lying around, waiting to be picked up. I've made over a hundred dollars in a week. Lots of the kids around here make extra money the easy way. You'd be surprised."

"I don't believe it."

"Ask some of the guys like Billy and Richard," Dudley said. "They work the carousel. They make at least twenty-five dollars a week."

"Mr. Fattooka pays them that much?"

"Of course not. They get a dollar a day just like everyone else. But like I said, they earn extra money because they know the angles."

"What angles are you talking about?" Adam asked. Then suddenly he remembered what Mary had said about the kids stealing money. He stared at Dudley in surprise. The older boy smiled knowingly.

"Frank and I could show you how to make a lot of money, kid," Dudley said.

"You mean steal it," Adam said angrily.

"You mean to tell me you've never stolen anything?" Dudley asked.

Adam was about to deny that he had when he vividly remembered taking Benjamin's money and candy bar out of his cousin's closet. He looked down at the ground. He was silent.

"I thought so," Dudley smirked. "I bet you've taken lots of stuff."

"I haven't taken lots," Adam insisted. "Just a little."

"Little by little it all adds up," Dudley said with a knowing grin. "You get used to it. It's sort of fun, like a game."

"I don't want any part of it. I'm not a thief. Well, at least not in the way you mean."

"I suppose you'd rather clean out pigpens all day the rest of your life," Dudley replied. "I thought you were smarter than that."

"You could really get in trouble stealing from people." Adam angrily scooped up another load of muck and threw it into the wheelbarrow.

"You're already in trouble," Dudley said. "But a smart kid doesn't get caught or get in trouble. Just think about it while you're shoveling all these barns, farm boy. There will be just as many in the next town. Have fun."

The older boy smiled and sauntered away. Adam seethed as he began scooping out the next stall. He pushed the edge of the big scoop shovel across the ground until it was full of old straw and mud and manure.

"Why did I ever end up here?" Adam muttered to himself. "I should just take off in the middle of the night. Nothing could be worse than this job."

Just as Adam began to think of a way to escape, Mr. Fattooka walked into the long barn. He wore his big white apron and carried an orange.

Adam pushed the scoop shovel a little faster as the big man walked over and stopped. Adam felt very uncomfortable being watched.

Mr. Fattooka stared at Adam. He took a black pocketknife out of his pocket. He unfolded a small, sharp blade and cut a small hole into the skin of the orange. He folded the blade back into place and stuck it in his pocket. He smiled at Adam as he held the orange up to his mouth. His thick lips covered the hole in the peel. His big hairy fist closed around the fruit, slowly squeezing and squeezing, sucking out all the juice, until all that remained was a crushed handful of peel and pulp. He looked disgusted as he threw the pulpy, wet mess on the dirt at Adam's feet.

"You aren't going to try to get out of paying that money you owe me, are you kid?" Mr. Fattooka asked. He wiped his wet hands on his apron. "I heard some talk that you weren't happy about your job."

"No, sir, of course not," Adam said, his voice trembling.

Mr. Fattooka took out his black pocketknife. He opened the larger blade. He carefully scraped underneath his thumbnail. His dark eyes looked at Adam again.

"We have a deal, then," the fat man said, tapping the blade in his big hand. "You're going to work for me until what you owe is paid off, right?"

"Uh, yes sir." Adam looked at the shiny blade of the knife. "Uh, how long do you think that will take? I mean, I was heading out to Seattle to live with my aunt and I don't want her to worry about me when I don't arrive on—"

"Seattle!" The huge man roared with laughter. He laughed so hard his eyes got wet. "You better write your aunt a letter and tell her you'll be delayed in your journey."

"Write a letter?" Adam asked.

"You can tell her you have a good summer job and won't be coming right away," the big man said seriously. "Maybe you'll work through the fall too. We have a heavy schedule down south in September and October, though not as busy as it used to be since the war started."

"Until October?" Adam asked. "But that's months from now!"

"You got to pay your bills, kid," the big man said. "No one cheats Fattooka. One boy tried one time. He tried to run away. But I went after him. He regretted making such a stupid decision. I got every penny that foolish boy owed me. No one cheats me. Now it's time to get back to work. The way you're talking and wasting time, I might need you through December."

Adam leaned on his shovel. The smell was awful. He scooped up the mess of orange peel and threw it in the wheelbarrow. He sighed and leaned over and began shoveling out the rest of the stall.

# PLANNING
# REVENGE

# 14

Adam cleaned stalls the next two days. The pile of manure and slop in the pit grew to the size of a small mountain. Adam worked steadily each day, shoveling the stalls, carrying it away, then bringing in fresh dirt and straw. By the end of the third day, Adam was totally sick of cleaning the stalls.

Each day, Dudley would stop by and poke fun at Adam for having the worst job at the carnival. Then he would offer to teach Adam how to pick pockets and steal. Adam refused, but he began to wonder. Dudley made it seem so easy.

Adam's arms and back ached more and more at the end of each day.

He had never worked so hard in his life doing something so unpleasant. The smell was terrible, and it just seemed to get worse.

He stayed in the big blue trailer with the rest of the kids. The boys stayed in one end of the trailer, and the girls stayed in the other. All the bunk beds were three beds high. Adam had the lower bunk, Danny, Mary's brother, had the middle bunk and an older boy named Richard was on top. Danny was a nice boy, but Adam didn't trust Richard, since he was Dudley's pal.

"I don't see how you can stand shoveling that stuff," Richard said as they got up the next morning.

"Since this is the last day of the fair, at least I'll be done," Adam said flatly.

"Mr. Fattooka will have you doing it in the next town," Richard replied as he pulled on his shoes. "He had a kid named Orville cleaning stalls for a month. Then the kid got sick and left when the carnival left that town. Then Max did it. But he got smart. He works at the Ring Toss booth now."

"How did he get out of it?" Adam asked.

"Like I said, he got smart," Richard replied. "He started helping Dudley. After he learned how, he started making good money. Not as much as Dudley. Nobody makes as much as him."

"I'm not a thief," Adam insisted as he put on his smelly shoes. No matter how much he cleaned them the night before, in the morning they still smelled like a pigpen. Adam crinkled his nose in disgust.

"You get used to it." Richard grinned. "I know I did."

"I'm not a thief," Adam repeated.

"You think you're better than the rest of us?" Richard demanded sourly.

"I didn't say that."

"You didn't have to," the older boy said. "Dudley says you act high and mighty for somebody who shovels manure all day. He says he might bring you down a peg. He knows just how to do it too."

"I'm not afraid of Dudley," Adam retorted. "He just talks big."

"You'll be sorry you said that," Richard replied. "I'm going to tell him what you said."

"Go ahead," Adam said as if he didn't care.

Richard laughed and left. Danny, who had been listening, hopped down from his bunk.

"I'd watch out for Dudley," Danny said seriously. "He can be really mean when he wants. I never cross him."

"I'm not trying to make him mad," Adam explained. "I just don't want to join their ring of thieves."

"They've never asked me to join in with them, at least not yet," Danny said. "Mr. Fattooka likes to keep Mary and me in the kitchen, so Dudley doesn't bother us."

"They say I could make enough money to pay Mr. Fattooka off in a couple of weeks," Adam said. "I'd like to pay him off and get out of this place. I feel like I've been stuck here forever."

"You will be stuck with him forever if you start stealing for him," Danny whispered. He looked around to make sure no one was listening. Most of the other boys had left the trailer.

"What do you mean?" Adam asked.

"I've overheard them talking," Danny said in a soft voice. "Once they start stealing, Mr. Fattooka really has them. I heard Richard talk about it soon after he got here. He said he took a man's wallet and gave it to Dudley, who gave it to Mr. Fattooka. They kept the money, but they also kept the wallet. Mr. Fattooka told Richard if he ever tried to run he would give the wallet to the police and tell them that Richard stole it."

"You mean he blackmails them so they have to keep working for him?" Adam asked.

"Sure. Why do you think all these kids stay here? None of them have left, except Max, and he was sick. But he never worked for Dudley. All these guys have been here since Mary and I started working. If they were making so much money, you'd think they save it up and take off. But they don't leave. They're all scared to leave, I think."

"That's not right!" Adam said fiercely. "They can't get away with that. It's against the law to blackmail people."

"It's against the law to steal too, but they get away with it," Danny said.

"Someone should tell the police or something."

"Not me," Danny said. "I'm not going to make waves. Mr. Fattooka would cut your tongue out if he found out you went to the police. And don't tell anyone I've told you this stuff. I'd be in big trouble."

"I won't tell," Adam promised. "We better go eat, or we won't get any breakfast."

The two boys ran to the food tent. Adam and Danny ate at the table with the other kids. Richard sat next to Dudley at the adults' table, talking up a storm. Adam wondered what Richard was saying. Dudley looked up at Adam more than once and just stared. Adam shifted uneasily in his seat. He finished breakfast quickly and left.

After most of the kids left, Mr. Fattooka walked over and sat down by Dudley. The big man did not look happy. He spoke to Dudley in a foreign language and Dudley answered back in the same language. The big man was plainly unhappy and Dudley was defensive.

"I can't help it!" Dudley said in English. "I've talked to him and he won't break. He'd rather shovel that manure all day. He's an idiot farm boy."

"I don't like it," Mr. Fattooka grunted. "A boy like that can be dangerous. He's too independent. We've got to break him like you break a wild horse."

"I told you I'm working on him."

"I want him working like the others."

"Why don't you just let him go when we leave tonight?" Dudley asked. "I know he hates working in the barns. He'd be glad to get out of here."

"Because he knows too much," the big man replied, pulling on his mustache. "And I don't trust him. He's the kind of kid who could cause trouble. Even Esmerelda told me so."

"That witch?" Dudley said in disgust. "She couldn't read the future even if she had tomorrow's newspaper right in front of her nose. You know she's a fake."

Without a word, the fat man slapped Dudley hard on the side of the face. The boy tripped backward across a table and landed on the ground. He got up slowly, rubbing the large red mark on his cheek.

"Don't you be fresh with me or your aunt Esmerelda," the big man said. "She has powers, I tell you. She said that boy made her nervous, that he had a bad spirit about him. She said he could bring bad luck."

Mr. Fattooka began talking in a foreign language again, yelling at Dudley. The boy with red hair didn't argue this time. He rubbed his stinging cheek and listened without saying a word.

Out at the barns, Adam pushed the wheelbarrow back and forth to the slop pile. He worked steadily all morning, ate lunch and went back to pushing the wheelbarrow again. The only good thing about the day was that a brisk breeze made the afternoon less hot. Even so, Adam was weary from the hard work.

"I should have gone back to Uncle Jacob's farm when I had the chance," Adam thought to himself as he dumped the wheelbarrow off the ramp. "Now it's too late. If I leave, I'll get in trouble. No one knows I'm here. I bet they're worrying. No matter what I do, I cause trouble."

As he started down the ramp, he saw a familiar figure waiting. Adam pushed the wheelbarrow more slowly. The ghost boy had grown as tall as an adult. "You deserve better than this slop. You should get smart, like Dudley said. He lives a nice comfortable life. He gets everything he wants. You could live like that."

"I'm no thief," Adam said hotly.

"Oh, no?" the ghost boy replied. He reached over and grabbed the chain of beads around Adam's neck. He tugged it softly. The guilt and shame Adam felt suddenly increased.

"I'm going to pay Benjamin back," Adam insisted.

"Sure you are. It will take you three months to pay off Mr. Fattooka."

"I'll pay him back after that."

"I would go for the easy money like Dudley said." The ghost boy yanked on the chain harder. Adam bent down, feeling the pain in his neck. The chain seemed heavier than ever. The beads seemed to have grown in the night. They were bigger than baseballs.

"You disgust me," the ghost boy said. "I'm only trying to help, and you act dumb. Wise up for a change."

"This whole place is disgusting." Adam threw down his shovel. "I hate it. I don't know how I ended up here."

"Get used to it. You're going to be here a long time."

Adam was about to reply when the ghostly figure disappeared. Adam grunted and then picked up the wheelbarrow. He looked sadly down at the heavy beads around his neck and felt sorry for himself. Then, for a moment, he saw it. Shining underneath the heavy dark beads was the golden key. Adam touched it.

"I keep forgetting about this for some reason," Adam said softly. He turned the little key over in his fingers. "I wish I could find a way out of this mess." The key seemed to shine even brighter. For a moment, Adam felt hopeful that he could get out of the jam he was in. He didn't know how, but he hoped it was possible.

"You, there!" a voice shouted out, interrupting his thoughts. Adam looked up.

A big black truck pulled up next to the row of parked trailers and trucks. *Goliath Toys* was painted in white letters on the side of the truck. The window on the driver's side was open. The truck stopped.

"Wait there, boy," the driver called out. A man dressed in a black suit got out of the truck. He wore a neat black derby on top of his head. He held a clipboard in his hands. He walked quickly toward Adam.

"Grinsby's my name, young fella." The man slightly tipped his derby. "I'm looking for a Mr. Herod Fattooka, the owner of this carnival. I have some toys for him."

"Toys for Mr. Fattooka?" Adam asked in surprise.

"Dolls, stuffed animals, prizes and so forth for his game booths." Mr. Grinsby smiled. "Carnival supplies and merchandise."

"Oh. He's usually at the food shack." Adam pointed in the direction of the midway.

"Thank you." The man turned and left. Adam pushed the wheelbarrow back to the barns. He was just pushing out another wheelbarrow load to the big pit when Mr. Fattooka, Frank and Dudley returned with the man named Grinsby. They went into Mr. Fattooka's fancy trailer. As Adam was dumping the wheelbarrow, Mr. Grinsby and the others came outside. They walked over to the black Goliath Toys truck. Adam rolled the wheelbarrow near the back of the truck and stopped. He stayed out of sight. He could hear the others inside the truck.

"I have all the usual supplies, of course, just as you ordered," Mr. Grinsby was saying. "Two dozen boxes of dolls, four dozen boxes of teddy bears, fifteen dozen boxes of blow-out whistles, etc. Oh, yes. A new box of crystal balls. Your Esmerelda must be awful careless to break so many of those."

"She has lots of help," Dudley said laughing. Mr. Fattooka laughed too.

"The cost on those went up to one dollar apiece, as you'll see on the invoice," Mr. Grinsby said.

"One dollar for a crystal ball!" roared Mr. Fattooka. "But the last time they were just fifty cents."

"There's a war on, Mr. Fattooka," Grinsby said crisply. "Everything's harder to get and costs more. That's why you should sell your business to Goliath Toys. We can make you a very fair offer."

"What is this very fair offer?" the big man grunted. "We can go to my trailer to talk."

"I think you'll be very impressed," Grinsby said eagerly.

Adam started pushing the wheelbarrow quickly away from the truck. He didn't want to be caught eavesdropping. He was halfway to the cow stalls when Mr. Fattooka and Grinsby and the others emerged from the back of the truck.

"One dollar apiece for crystal balls!" Adam exclaimed under his breath. "And they told me they cost one hundred dollars. He's been lying to me all this time!"

Frank and Dudley began carrying boxes and boxes of toys and other merchandise from the black truck to a big blue truck parked next to Mr. Fattooka's trailer. Mr. Fattooka and Mr. Grinsby watched. Adam wheeled another load of slop over to the pile as Dudley and Frank carried a long wooden crate out of the truck which said *Crystal Balls, Future Glass Works, 2 Dozen*. No one seemed to even notice Adam. When the truck was empty, Grinsby got back inside and drove away.

"They can't get away with that!" Adam said angrily as Mr. Fattooka and the others walked back to the midway. "I've got to do something. But what? I'll get even with that liar and make him pay!"

Adam kept cleaning the stalls, planning on how he would confront Mr. Fattooka. He would demand to be paid his money for three days' work and then he would leave. Mr. Fattooka couldn't do anything about it.

Mary brought him supper around six-thirty in the evening. Adam told her about the accident and breaking the crystal ball. Then he told her about Grinsby's visit. "And they pretended that those crystal balls cost a hundred dollars," Adam said angrily. "But they only cost one buck!"

"He told us they cost a hundred and twenty-five dollars." Mary frowned.

"You mean you broke a crystal ball?"

"Danny did. He was helping Stump carry Esmerelda's table, just like you, in the freak house. Mr. Fattooka told us never to tell anyone what happened."

"I bet he's tricked other kids the same way," Adam fumed. "I'm really going to fix him. He can't just cheat people like that."

"But how?" Mary asked. "He so big and mean."

"I don't know, but I'll think of a way," Adam said with determination.

"It will be dark soon. I'll clean a little longer and think of a plan. Then we'll get him. We'll make him pay back everything he owes."

"Be careful," Mary warned. "I better get back or he'll be mad."

Mary left quickly. Adam started cleaning the next stall. He grumbled and fumed as he filled the wheelbarrow. He turned to push the wheelbarrow outside, but was blocked by a big red bicycle. Adam was glad for a second, then he frowned when he heard the soft words of the Prince.

"Get back on the path," the voice said so quietly he almost couldn't hear it.

"But I've got to get that rat Fattooka," Adam said. "I'm going to fix him."

"Revenge is mine," the voice said. "Get back on the path."

"Leave me alone." Adam angrily pushed the wheelbarrow past the bicycle. "I'll take care of this business. Then I'll go back."

Adam pushed the wheelbarrow with great determination down through the center of the barn. He kept thinking he would hear the words of the Prince again, but he didn't. The boy stopped and turned around. The old red bicycle was gone. Adam blinked in surprise. He felt uneasy as he pushed the wheelbarrow outside.

"I'm not afraid of that big goon," the boy said hotly, trying to build up his courage. "If he tries to threaten me, I'll threaten him right back. He'll be sorry he ever messed with me."

"You can't outsmart Mr. Fattooka," a voice said behind him. Adam whirled around. He expected to see the Prince, but it was the ghost boy sitting on a corral gate, bigger than ever, and he appeared to be very scared.

Adam frowned and kept pushing the wheelbarrow. "I'll tell the police." He tried to ignore the ghostly figure. "I'll call the FBI. That skunk can't get away with this."

"But he's an adult," the ghost boy said. "They'll believe him and not you."

"Shut up!" Adam pushed the wheelbarrow outside to the pit, trying to ignore the ghostly figure. But the ghost boy stuck to him like his shadow. Adam pushed faster, leaning into a stiff breeze that was blowing across the field.

"I wouldn't make waves if I were you," the ghost boy warned as Adam pushed the empty wheelbarrow down the ramp. "Besides, you've already got enough trouble right now."

"What do you mean?" Adam demanded.

"You've got company coming, and they don't look too friendly." The ghost boy looked in the direction of the midway. Across the field, Dudley and Richard and several other boys pointed at Adam. They walked straight toward him. None of the boys were smiling. Dudley bent down and picked up a big rock. The other boys did the same. When their hands were full of rocks, they suddenly spread out in a big half circle. On Dudley's signal, they began closing in around Adam.

# THE CAGE
# ON THE SLOP
# PILE
# 15

**It was too** late for Adam to run. The ramp and pit full of manure were behind him. The boys moved in faster, cutting off any way of escape. Dudley smiled. A sudden gust of wind blew his red hair into a wild mess.

"I hear you've been talking real high and mighty and making threats behind my back," Dudley said loudly so he could be heard above the wind. "You think you're better than the rest of us guys."

"I didn't say I was better than you," Adam replied.

"Richard said you were acting real tough this morning before breakfast," Dudley said. "He said you called me a chicken and a coward."

"I didn't say that!" Adam said.

"You did too," Richard accused. "You're just lying now because you're talking to Dudley face to face."

"I never called you a chicken," Adam repeated. He flinched as the other boys moved closer.

"You shouldn't call me names behind my back," Dudley said. He walked over until he was right in front of Adam. "You need to apologize to me, right now."

"I never called you a chicken." Adam could feel his face turning red.

Without warning, Dudley swung his fist into Adam's stomach. Adam gasped as he fell to his knees, trying to catch his breath. It felt like a horse had kicked him in the stomach. Adam felt tears coming to his eyes.

"Get up, you crybaby," Dudley hissed. "You still need to apologize."

"I . . . didn't . . . call . . . you . . . a chicken," Adam gasped.

"What should we do with this crybaby liar?" Dudley asked the other boys. "Should we let him run and then use our rocks? Or just pound him into the ground right where he sits?"

"Let's use him for target practice," Richard said. "We can pretend he's a Nazi tank and blast him to smithereens."

"That's not a bad idea." The red-haired boy looked at the long ramp leading up to the manure pit. He smiled broadly. "But I've got a better idea. Let's make him walk the plank. Just like we're at sea. Only this will be over that pile of slop he loves so much."

"Walk the plank! Walk the plank!" the boys all yelled. "Make the crybaby walk the plank!"

Dudley and Richard pulled Adam to his feet. Adam tried to jerk his arms free, but the bigger boys were stronger. The other boys crowded in as they pushed Adam up the wooden ramp that led over the manure pit.

"Walk the plank! Walk the plank!" they chanted as they pushed him along.

"You won't mind taking a little swim, will you?" Dudley asked. He grinned at the other boys. "He loves this stuff. He's been shoveling it for days now."

"Walk the plank! Walk the plank!" the boys shouted louder.

"Noooooo!" Adam yelled as they got to the end of the ramp. Dudley punched him in the stomach again. As he bent over, Richard and the other boys pushed all at once. Adam yelled out as his feet left the ramp. He clawed at the air helplessly as he fell face down. He held his arms in front of him, trying to break the fall. But his arms quickly sank down into the soft gushy pile as the rest of his body hit with a sickening slap. Adam closed his mouth as his face hit the slop.

Hitting the soft wet pile stung, but not as badly as he had anticipated. The smell was the worst. He was totally covered with the wet sticky mess. He sat up, wiping his eyes and mouth, trying to get it off. Up above, Dudley and the other boys cheered and howled with laughter.

"That will teach you to think you're so high and mighty," Dudley shouted down at Adam.

"We should make him the new exhibit at the freak show," Richard yelled. "He could stay in Sarx's cage. We could call him Adam the Slophead!"

The other boys laughed and began calling him more ugly names. Some of the boys cursed at him.

"You better learn who is boss around here, Slophead," Dudley called down. "When I tell you to come work for me, you better do it or you'll get a lot worse than this, do you hear?"

Adam nodded breathlessly. He was still trying to wipe the brown and green smelly glop off his arms and face. The boys up above laughed and hollered as they walked back down the ramp. But even when they were finally gone, Adam could still hear their insults and taunts ringing in his ears.

"I'll get them," Adam whimpered. He had felt bad the last several days, but this was the absolute worst. No matter which way he moved,

he was stuck in the stinking mountain of slop. Wherever he put his foot or hand, it sank down in the muddy wet pile. The suction then made it hard to move or pull away.

Adam sighed and sat back in the pile, trying to collect his thoughts. He felt so heavy and alone and humiliated. He grabbed for the baseball-sized beads around his neck. Adam rubbed one bitterly.

"I hate you!!!!" he screamed at the sky. He wasn't sure who he was screaming at, but he had to scream. The wind suddenly blew stronger around him. Adam's anger was so strong, he felt like he would explode. "It's not fair, it's not fair, it's not fair," Adam yelled. "None of this is fair!"

He yanked off one of the heavy dark beads from the chain around his neck and threw it into the wind, as if trying to hit some unseen tormentor. But the bead was heavier than a shot put and fell a few feet away, sinking deep into the pile of slop. For some reason, this made Adam even angrier. He pulled off another bitter bead and threw it into the wind. Again the bead fell far short of his expectations. It sank down into the brown and green ooze with a hopeless plop.

Like a wild man in a frenzy, Adam plucked the heavy dark beads one by one and tried to throw them far away, but all of them landed nearby, making a deep hole in the muck. He spun in a crazy circle, bitterly throwing out the beads, trying to rid himself of their weight.

"I can't do anything," Adam said with dejection. He struggled to his feet. The wind, which had been getting stronger by the second, suddenly blew the boy back over. Adam sat down hard. The wind whipped around him faster and faster, picking up bits of straw and dirt and leaves. Adam watched in fear and surprise as the wind twisted even harder and faster.

"It's a whirlwind!" Adam realized, holding up his arm to shield his eyes. He struggled to his feet. The wind only blew harder. Like a tiny tornado, the whirlwind hovered over the manure pit, spinning and turning. With his forearm over his face, Adam opened his eyes a crack. He found himself in the center of the spinning whirlwind.

Without warning, a large round bar of steel suddenly shot up into the air out of the pile of slop. Adam leaned backward and almost fell over. Behind him, another dark heavy bar whooshed straight up out of the pile, then another and another and another. All around him bars shot up into the air.

The whirlwind died down almost as quickly as it had come, but the bars stood high in the air. Adam stared at the bars closely. He was totally surrounded by them. Each of them had shot up out of the slop pile precisely where one of the dark heavy beads had fallen. Like deathly seeds, the bitter beads had grown up into hard metal bars. Dozens of the bars surrounded the boy like a circular jail or cage. Only this jail had no door. Adam began to feel worried.

"What is this thing?" he asked fearfully. He struggled to his feet again and slogged over to the bars. He reached out to touch one, but it was freezing cold. The bar turned the moisture on his hand to ice.

The touch of the bar lingered on his hand. As clearly as yesterday, he saw himself crying in the bed in Benjamin's bedroom. It was the first night he had arrived at Uncle Jacob's farm. His loud cries echoed through the bars.

Adam stumbled backward and hit another freezing cold bar. He suddenly saw a dark night with bombs exploding in fire and thunder on a darkened city. His whole body was filled with fear over the fate of his parents.

"Don't let them die over there," Adam whimpered. He shook his head, trying to make the picture go away. "Mommy and Daddy, please come home."

The frightful memory slowly faded, and Adam found himself inside the cage once more, knee deep in the manure pile. "What's happening to me?" Adam asked, looking at the bars in wonder. Touching the bars was like touching the heavy bitter beads, only the feelings were now so much worse. On each bar he could see writing. He leaned closer to read it. Each bar had his name on it, and after his name was a date and a few words of description. The one he had touched last said: "John Adam Kramar: May 23rd—Bombing in London—fear of parents dying."

He stared at the bars. One said, "July 16th—Tractor wreck—fear of punishment, shame, insults and anger at cousins." He looked at another bar next to it, "July 15th—Dead tree—fear of falling—anger and insults at cousins."

Adam looked at each bar until he got tired of reading them. Each one made him remember something from his past which he wished he could forget. Now they were more present than ever, like shadows made of steel. One after another after another, the bars totally closed him inside. He was surrounded and locked in by bars of hatred, shame, fear, anger and bitter memories.

Adam sat down helplessly in the middle of his cage planted in the pile of slimy muck. In the distance, he could hear the noises of the fair and people having fun.

"What kind of journey is this?" Adam asked bitterly. "I'm not going anywhere. Is this where I was supposed to end up? I came this far so I could be stuck in this slop pile? This just isn't fair."

He felt himself slowly sinking deeper and deeper into the ooze, as the sun fell below the horizon. Not far away, a family was walking across the field toward the parking lot. There was a mother and father and two children holding balloons and prizes. They were all smiling and laughing and talking. Then the little girl noticed Adam.

"Look at that boy, Daddy," the little girl said. "Why is he sitting on top of that big pile?"

"That's odd," the man said. The whole family stopped and looked at Adam curiously. Adam felt like some kind of beast on display in the zoo or like Sarx in his cage.

"Yuck. That must be awful stinky," the boy said. "Why doesn't he come down?"

"Do you need help to get down from there, young fella?" the man asked Adam.

"There's no way through the bars," Adam said miserably. "I can't get out."

"What bars, mama?" the little girl asked. "Do you see any bars?"

"I don't see any bars," the boy added. "What's he talking about?"

"I'm not sure," the woman said with a frown. "He must be confused. Maybe you should go get a policeman, Herbert."

The parents looked worried and a little afraid as they stared at Adam. The mother pulled her daughter back a step, as if trying to protect her.

"I'm sure that boy will come down when he's ready," the man said.

"Help me!" Adam cried out.

"Come along, children," the man said. "This is none of our business." He pulled his son by the hand and continued walking toward the parking lot. The rest of the family followed.

"Can't you help me?" Adam yelled after them.

The family kept walking as if they hadn't heard. The little girl looked back over her shoulder at Adam. She stuck out her tongue at him and turned back around. The family disappeared in the rows of cars in the parking lot.

"They won't help you. No one's going to help you," a voice said behind him. Adam looked around. The ghost boy was now at least ten feet tall. He stood inside the cage, grinning from ear to ear. "This is the end of the line, kid, the last stop. Your journey's over, pal. You and me are together at last."

The ghost boy laughed. Under his arm, he held the black box. The sides flashed and danced with mysterious lights. The ghostly figure saw Adam looking at it.

"Want this?" he taunted. He lifted the lid an inch. Blue smoke poured out. In spite of everything, Adam was instantly curious. The ghostly giant leaned forward, offering it to Adam. "I guess you've finally won it."

"Good, because I haven't won anything else at this stupid carnival," Adam said. He took the box with his messy hands. He quickly opened the lid. Smoke continued to pour out. Adam coughed and waved his arms. When the smoke cleared, he looked inside. He reached in with his hand and pulled out a fistful of gray powder.

"Ashes." Adam threw them away. He frantically reached again and brought out another fistful of the gray powder. "It's only ashes!"

"That's your big prize, kid." The ghostly giant grinned. "That's all you'll ever get. Today is your lucky day, all right. Have fun."

The ghostly giant roared with laughter as Adam threw the box down in disgust. He sat down in the pile of muck and put his face in his hands. Time seemed to have stopped and left him trapped. Adam didn't try to escape or even think of trying to escape. He looked at the bars as if they were the walls of his home and final resting place.

"Why do you stay in that cage?" a child's voice asked. Outside the cage, two boys and a little girl were sitting on big red bicycles. The children couldn't have been older than second graders. They stared curiously at Adam.

"I can't leave," Adam said miserably. "I deserve to be here, I guess."

"That's not what he said," the littlest boy said. "He told us to let you out so you could go home and get back on the path."

"Get back on the path?" Adam repeated. "Who told you that?"

"The Prince, of course," the little boy said. "He told us to come here and let you out because you forgot how to use your key."

"I have mine." The little girl smiled. She reached down toward her heart and lifted up a shining golden key that was connected to a thin golden chain. Her big red bike started to roll. The tires lifted quietly up into the air. She glided up over the pile of slop near the bars. She held out the key and touched the closest bar.

The whole cage flashed and sizzled, as angry sparks jumped like lightning around the bars. The bars glowed red and the space between them widened. She flew into the opening of the cage.

"Hop on," the little girl said.

"But I'll get your bike all messy and yucky," Adam said shamefully. "And it smells awful."

"We'll wash it off," she replied with a smile. "Hop on!"

Adam climbed on the back of the old bike. Immediately the bike shot through the opening in the bars. Adam and the little girl soared upward, away from the stinking pile of slop. The two little boys flew up in the air by Adam and the little girl.

They glided across the field to the sheep and goat barn, landing on the ground near the faucet with the black hose.

"I've been here before," Adam said as he climbed off the bicycle. It seemed like weeks, instead of days ago, that he had crashed in the pigpen and had needed to hose off.

One of the little boys turned on the hose as the other aimed it at Adam. The cool water felt wonderfully refreshing. Adam got totally soaked from head to toe. Little by little, all the smelly slop washed off.

"Thanks," Adam said with a grin. He was dripping water everywhere.

"Your Spirit Flyer is here." The little girl pointed over by the shed. Adam saw the old bike. Part of him felt glad to see it, but another part felt uneasy.

"You are supposed to get on your bike and let it take you back to the path," said the little boy holding the hose.

"No way," Adam said. "I'm going to change clothes. Then I'm going to get even with Dudley and Mr. Fattooka. I'm going to make them wish they never messed with me."

"But the Prince said you should get back on the path," the little girl said. "The cage can still capture you, he said. We all heard him."

"I will get back on the path," Adam said with renewed determination. "Just as soon as I get even with those guys. Thanks for helping me out."

Adam started walking toward the trailer. The three children looked at each other with puzzled expressions. They ran after Adam.

"But your Spirit Flyer is waiting for you," the little girl said. "You should go now before it's too late."

"Too late for what?" Adam asked. He was starting to get annoyed with the kids tagging along behind him. In the distance, lightning flashed and the sky rumbled. "You kids better get home. Looks like it's going to rain."

"You need to get back on the path, or you'll get stuck again," one of the boys warned. "The cage isn't gone."

"Later," Adam replied. He ducked into the trailer and slammed the door shut behind him, hoping the kids would get the message to leave him alone.

The trailer was empty. He quickly changed into dry clothes. He opened the trailer door a crack. The little kids were gone, so Adam went outside in the night air, ready to get even.

# ADAM
# FINDS HIS
# WALLET
· · · · · · · ·
# 16

Adam hadn't taken two steps before rain
began to fall. He frowned at the sky. Lightning flashed far away in the
west, and the air was soon filled with the rumbling thunder.

"At least this will give me an excuse not to push the wheelbarrow
anymore tonight." Adam pulled up his collar and ran toward the midway. Crowds of people were hurriedly leaving the fair because of the
rain. Some of the fair workers were busily taking down the exhibit
booths so they could load them up and move to the next town.

Adam ran to the food shack. He stopped to look and see who was
inside. He didn't see Mr. Fattooka or Dudley. Adam ran into the shack

and hurried over to Mary. She smiled when she saw him. Danny walked over too.

"We're going to close down and get ready to move," Mary said. "We open in Centerville tomorrow afternoon."

"Centerville?" Adam asked. "I didn't know that was the next stop. I have to talk to Mr. Fattooka."

"He's gone," Mary said. "I saw him and Dudley and Frank leave together. We're probably going to close early tonight because of the rain. They had problems with the wiring in the freak show exhibit and already closed it for the night."

"They went to count up their money," Danny said. "I heard Mr. Fattooka talking to Dudley."

"Where do they go?" Adam demanded impatiently. "I'm going to tell Mr. Fattooka what I know and make him pay me for all my work."

"They'll be in their fancy trailer," Danny said. "I want to get back at him just as much as you. Mary told me everything you talked about. He's a bigger crook than I ever imagined."

"Let's go then," Adam said. "I'm going to make him sorry he ever lied to me."

"Follow me." Danny took off his apron and threw it on the counter.

"Be careful!" Mary warned.

Adam followed the younger boy through the rain. They ran back to the rows of trucks and trailers at the edge of the fairgrounds.

"The light is on, so they must be there," Danny said and pointed. The two boys crept through the darkness toward the big trailer. Light came from a small window at the end of the trailer. As they got closer, they heard voices.

Adam raised his head slowly, peeking through the window. At one side of the trailer, all the people from the freak show were playing poker. The fat couple, the tall thin man, the woman with a beard, and Stump, the dwarf, were all holding cards and making bets.

At the other end of the trailer, Adam saw Mr. Fattooka, Dudley and

Frank walking into another room. They closed the door behind them.

"I can't see Fattooka from here," Adam whispered to Danny. The two boys crept down the side of the trailer. When they got to another window, Adam raised his head and looked inside. Fattooka and the others sat around a big table that was piled with wallets, a few purses and stacks of cash. Adam saw a brown wallet with black stitching and a large K embossed on the side.

"My wallet," Adam hissed softly.

"This was a good week." Mr. Fattooka looked at the pile on the table. "Too bad the rain's going to shut us down early tonight."

"Like you say, last nights are the best pickings," Dudley said with a grin.

"I can't believe that goon from Goliath Toy Company thinks I'm going to sell him my midway," the big man grunted. "He only offered me half what this carnival is worth. Then he starts making his stupid threats."

"He doesn't look like a guy who will take no for an answer," Frank said cautiously. "He doesn't scare easily."

"Fattooka doesn't scare at all," the big man said angrily. "This Grinsby talks big and makes his threats. He said he would bring his friends while we were at Centerville. Next time I see him I'll teach him some respect."

Dudley laughed, nodding his head. Mr. Fattooka stood up. He picked up the wallets and purses and put them in a large black trunk. He closed the lid and locked it with a padlock.

"We'll send these back to New York on the next truck and my cousin can sell them," the big man said.

"You're the smartest," Dudley grinned.

Just then, a loud popping noise echoed through the night from the direction of the midway. Mr. Fattooka and the others in the trailer heard it too, and headed for the door.

"Hide!" Adam hissed. He and Danny scooted underneath the trailer just as the door opened. They saw several pairs of legs hurry down the little set of steps.

"It sounds like a problem with the ferris wheel again," Frank said.

"We better check it," Mr. Fattooka snarled. They all started to run for the midway. Adam and Danny waited until they were far ahead, then scooted out from underneath the trailer.

"That was close," Danny whispered.

"Let's see what's going on," Adam said.

The two boys trotted toward the midway. The rain began to fall harder. Droves of people were leaving the fair. Adam slowed down as they passed the food shack.

Up ahead, there was a commotion around the ferris wheel. People were shouting and pointing. The big wheel had stopped, and half the riders were still up in the buckets, yelling and waving, trying to get out of the rain. Adam and Danny went closer. Fattooka was yelling at Frank, who was trying to move the big lever that started and stopped the wheel. The big engine roared loudly.

Suddenly, the ferris wheel lurched. Everyone screamed at once as the buckets rocked their passengers wildly. Frank pushed on the lever again and the wheel moved but made a loud grinding noise. Ever so slowly, the riders came down to the ramp. Dudley was there, helping them out. Adam and Danny moved closer.

"That big gear must have broken again," Danny said excitedly. "This is the second time it's happened!"

Adam looked where Danny was pointing. He saw a large crack in the metal. Frank was watching the crack, too, as he made the big wheel move. Bucket by bucket, the anxious riders got off the wheel. Finally everyone was off.

Several adults were crowded around Mr. Fattooka, pointing at the ferris wheel and talking angrily. The big man's arms were folded across his chest. Adam wanted to get closer to listen when he saw Dudley and Richard slink away from the crowd.

"Let's see what they're up to," Adam said to Danny.

Richard and Dudley walked straight for the carousel. Adam followed close behind. The spinning carousel slowed down. Several parents crowded up under the roof of the carousel to get out of the rain. When it stopped, there was lots of confusion as the adults tried to find their children.

That's when Dudley and Richard moved in. As a woman reached up to get her little boy from a horse, Dudley quickly reached into the woman's open purse and took out a small change purse that he stuffed neatly under his shirt. He walked over to Richard, who was holding a brown shopping bag. He dropped it into the bag and went back to the carousel. A man in overalls was trying to lead three little children through the crowd. Dudley bumped up against him. The man turned around, but Dudley had quickly sidestepped through the crowd. When he reached Richard, he dropped a black wallet into the bag and headed back for the carousel.

"Did you see that?" Adam asked indignantly.

Danny nodded. "He's really fast."

Dudley walked quickly out of the crowd and headed toward Richard. He dropped something into the paper bag.

"He did it again," Adam said. "This has got to stop."

Adam walked straight over to Dudley and Richard. The two boys were laughing. "I saw what you just did, and I'm going to tell the police right now," Adam loudly announced. "And I know you took my wallet too. I saw it a few minutes ago on the table in Mr. Fattooka's trailer. Danny saw it too. He's a witness."

"What are you talking about?" Dudley asked. He laughed, but he looked uncomfortable.

"Dudley didn't do nothing," Richard said.

"I saw it with my own eyes," Adam said angrily. "I saw my wallet on the table in Mr. Fattooka's trailer a few minutes ago. I know you stole my wallet the first day I came here when you gave me a free ride on the ferris wheel. You bumped into me and took it, just like you bumped into that man with three kids at the carousel just now.

You have his wallet in that bag."

Adam pointed at the brown paper sack. Richard looked at Dudley nervously. The boy with red hair stared at Adam with contempt.

"I also saw you steal something from a woman's purse at the carousel, too," Adam said. "I'm going to go get a policeman right now." Adam turned and ran straight into the big apron of Mr. Fattooka. He grabbed Adam by the arms and held him tight.

"Why aren't you working?" the fat man asked.

"This boy is a thief!" Adam said loudly. "He stole my wallet, and I'm telling the police. And I saw him stealing just now at the carousel. Now let me go!"

"Hold it!" Mr. Fattooka's big arms held Adam as tight as a vise. "There's no need to make a lot of noise. If Dudley took something from you, he'll return it."

"You bet he will," Adam spat out. "And what about that crystal ball? I happened to hear Mr. Grinsby say they cost one dollar, not one hundred dollars like you said. You owe me money for working like a slave for four days, and I want every penny of it, not to mention the money Dudley and you got from my wallet! I know exactly how much was there."

Mr. Fattooka turned and spoke softly to Dudley in a foreign language. Adam couldn't understand a word. Dudley spoke back slowly in the same language. He sounded angry. He pointed a finger at Adam and glared.

"We will go get your things right now," Mr. Fattooka said. "Dudley is very sorry about this misunderstanding. And so am I."

"You both better be," Adam snarled. "I want every dime that's coming to me. I know exactly how much I had. Then we'll go have a little talk with the police. I'm sure they'll be real interested in what's in that bag."

Adam pointed at the paper sack in Richard's hands. Mr. Fattooka held onto Adam with one hand and took the sack with the other. He looked in the bag and then looked at Adam curiously.

"Dudley will return these things," the big man said. "But first, we go over to the trailer and get your wallet and money."

"Danny is my witness, in case you two goons think you can lie your way out of this to the sheriff," Adam said.

"Danny?" the big man said. He looked at the younger boy with a scowl. "You go back to work now and help your sister. We set up at the fair in Centerville tomorrow."

"He also knows that you lied to him and Mary about the crystal ball," Adam said gleefully. "I'm telling the police how you cheated them too. You're going to be sorry you messed with me. Centerville may have to wait after we go talk to the sheriff," Adam insisted triumphantly.

"Go on now, Danny," Mr. Fattooka continued. "I'll talk to you later."

The younger boy trembled and then looked down at his feet. He shuffled slowly back over toward the food shack. Adam was surprised to watch him go.

"Danny?" Adam asked. The younger boy kept walking as if he hadn't heard.

"He's a smart boy," Fattooka said. "You're a smart boy too. Let's all go get your wallet. Then Dudley will apologize."

Mr. Fattooka held tightly onto Adam as they walked through the midway, past the animal barns to the edge of the fairgrounds where all the carnival trucks and trailers were parked. Dudley looked straight ahead.

"You're hurting my arm." Adam tried to jerk it free, but Mr. Fattooka was amazingly strong. The rain had slowed down.

"No need to be so angry, young man," Mr. Fattooka said in a friendly manner. "Dudley is sorry, I told you."

They walked over to Mr. Fattooka's trailer. A big truck with its lights on and engine running was parked in front of the trailer. The driver got out. He was laughing. He held a half-full bottle of whiskey in one hand and spoke in a foreign language to Mr. Fattooka. Mr. Fattooka did not smile. He took the bottle of whiskey away from the driver. The driver got angry and said something, but Mr. Fattooka slapped him with the back of his hand. The driver's head snapped back, his lip bleeding. Adam was surprised how hard Mr. Fattooka had hit the man. The driver mumbled something, but hurried back behind the steering wheel of the truck.

Adam began to feel very alone so far away from the midway and the crowds. "Let's get my wallet out of the trailer and go back to the food shack," Adam said uneasily. "I saw you put it in the trunk."

"Unfortunately, the trunk has already been loaded on this truck," the big man said. "That stupid driver is in a big hurry. On the last night of the fair, everyone wants to hurry and load up so we can get set up in Centerville early. You are in a hurry to get your wallet and go to the police. Everyone is in too much of a hurry."

Mr. Fattooka walked to the back of the truck and opened the big swinging doors. "Get in there and show this kid where to get his wallet, Dudley."

Dudley hopped up into the truck. Adam peered inside. There were all sorts of boxes and other things in the truck. In the back it was too dark to see. "The trunk's back here," Dudley said to Adam. "Come help me bring it out."

Adam hopped in. He walked slowly back behind the boxes into the darkness next to Dudley. "I don't see it." Adam was suspicious. "Let's go back to the food shack and settle this."

"The trunk is right there, behind that box," Dudley said. Adam took a step farther into the darkness.

"Where?" Adam asked, leaning forward.

"There!" Dudley said as he violently pushed Adam down.

Adam yelled, putting his arms out to try to catch his fall. A box crashed down on his head and then another. He struggled to his feet just in time to see the big back door swing shut.

"Let me out!" Adam screamed. In the darkness he heard the lock click shut. Adam stumbled in the direction of the door. He banged on it. He heard laughing outside.

"That'll teach that idiot tattletale," Dudley said.

"Come on," Mr. Fattooka said. "Marcus will take him to my cousin Franky when he gets to New York. Franky can put him to work in his fertilizer factory. And if he doesn't work, Franky will take care of this problem."

Adam heard more laughter, but it was drowned out as the truck began slowly moving away into the darkness.

# ASK

· · · · · · · ·

# 17

Adam worked his way to the front of the truck and tried pounding on the walls and yelling. But after five minutes, his throat and hands were sore, and he stopped. From the sound, Adam could tell they were riding fast down a highway by then. He found a box in the dark and sat down on it.

"It'll take two days at least to get to New York," Adam muttered to himself. "I can't believe I let them trick me again. I'm such an idiot! I could starve in here."

"You deserve it, you dummy," he heard a voice say in the dark. "You really goofed up. This time it's permanent. What if these guys put a chain around your neck and throw you in the river? You'll be one dead dummy then."

"They won't do that," Adam said out loud. "They won't really hurt me."

"These guys are criminals, stupid," the ghost boy said. "They know how to deal with fools like you."

Adam didn't respond. His eyes filled with tears in the back of the dark truck. He wiped them with his sleeve. He felt so scared and ashamed that he didn't know what to do. He shivered in the darkness, trying to get hold of himself.

"How could I be so stupid?" he asked himself over and over. "No one knows where I am. This is all my fault. How could I be so stupid, stupid, stupid?"

Adam looked up at the ceiling in the dark, wishing he might find some answer. The truck swayed gently as it rolled down the road. Adam groped around in the dark. The headlights of a car behind the truck shone through a crack in the back door long enough for Adam to explore. In the dim light he saw several large metal trunks that were locked with padlocks. Behind some cardboard boxes he saw a big wooden carousel horse missing a front and back leg. Next to that was a pile of packing blankets. Adam moved some boxes and spread out the blankets. He sat on them as he leaned against the side wall of the truck. The car behind the truck passed them and the back of the truck was dark once more.

"I wish I was out of here," Adam said softly. "I wish I was anywhere but here. Why didn't I leave when those kids told me to go? I must have been crazy! I should have known when my Spirit Flyer crashed the first time that there was something I wasn't doing right."

"That's the truth!" a voice echoed in the darkness of Adam's mind. "You never do anything right."

"Leave me alone," Adam said halfheartedly.

"You're stuck with me," the voice answered. "You never really changed, like they said. See, you're in a mess all over again. If you had changed, you wouldn't be here, would you?"

Adam didn't know what to say. The ghost slave sounded dreadfully convincing. Another car pulled up behind the truck. In the dim light, the boy saw the dark bars. Adam struggled to his feet and turned in a slow circle. The bars completely surrounded him, just like they had at the slop pit.

"It's come back," Adam moaned.

"We're together for good, this time," the ghostly figure announced. He smiled broadly in the dim light.

"They must think I'm dead by now," Adam whispered.

"That's for sure. They've given up on you forever. You made a big, final mistake this time. Three strikes and you're out, buddy. Out of the game."

"I wish I could do it all over," Adam said. "I shouldn't have run away. Why didn't I go back when I had the chance? I wish I had just gotten on my Spirit Flyer and left."

Adam looked at the bars helplessly. The car passed and the back of the truck was totally dark again. He sighed and sat back down on the blankets. He closed his eyes, wishing he could forget his way out of the whole situation. He leaned back on the blankets and drifted off into an uneasy sleep.

The truck went around a curve so fast that the tires squealed. Adam woke up with a start. He immediately remembered he was in the back of the truck. He wasn't sure how much time had passed. He moved his legs again, trying to get comfortable. As he moved, he saw a faint glow inside his shirt. Adam blinked in surprise. The glow was still there. He quickly unbuttoned the top buttons. His mouth dropped open when he saw it. The golden key was hanging on the thin golden chain.

Adam grabbed the key with both hands and held it up in front of his face. Even in the dark, he could still read his name in the shining key: John Adam Kramar. He flipped it over and saw one word: ASK.

"Ask," Adam said softly.

"Put that trinket away!" the ghost slave screeched nearby in the darkness. "You can't ask anything again. You're out of wishes, remember? You struck out!"

"Yeah." Adam almost stuck the key back inside his shirt, but the warm glow was too comforting. He held the key tightly. "I wish I could ask and he would listen again. I wish I had another chance."

As soon as the words left his lips, it happened. Suddenly the back of the truck was filled with light. The boy turned and saw the Prince sitting down three feet away inside the bars with him. The Prince smiled.

Adam was speechless. He leaned forward to bow. As he raised his head, he saw that he and the Prince were both sitting on royal golden chairs. Adam looked around. Even though he could tell he was in the back of the truck, Adam could faintly see towering palace walls and windows made of diamonds. For a moment, it seemed as if he were in two places at the same time: in the truck and in the Palace of the Kings.

"How can this be?" Adam asked.

"I've been sitting next to you all day," the Prince said with a smile. "You could have used your key any time."

"I could have?" Adam asked.

"I'm always with you," the Prince said. "If you use your key and ask, you'll find me. You'll open the doors to blessing and the gifts and riches of my Kingdom."

"But I thought I struck out," Adam said sheepishly. "I mean I've made such a big mess of things. I can't do anything right! I should have gone back to the path, but . . ."

Adam felt sorry for himself and started to make excuses, but looking into the eyes of the Prince, he knew he couldn't explain or lie his way out of what happened. And at the same time, he realized that he didn't need to lie or explain. The Prince already knew it all, yet he wasn't angry or upset. His magnificent eyes were full of kindness and concern.

"I'm sorry I messed up," Adam said softly. "I didn't obey you. I always mess up. I wish I could do it over."

Adam felt tears come to his eyes. More than anything, he was sorry because he felt like he had disappointed the Prince of Kings. The man in white robes did not hesitate. He pulled the sobbing boy gently into his arms and patted him on the back.

"I want you to finish this journey too," the Prince of Kings said softly. "And you shall."

"Really?" Adam asked.

The Prince nodded, and right before his eyes, he disappeared. The light faded away. Just as Adam's eyes got used to the darkness, he heard the screech of tires as the truck began to slide and sway in the road. Adam tried to steady himself, but slipped to one side. Then he heard the sound of crunching metal as the truck lurched to a stop.

Everything was suddenly still. Adam heard a door of the truck slam and a man cursing in the darkness. In the sudden stop, the back door rolled up a few inches, letting in a beam of light as a car pulled up from behind the truck and stopped. He heard more car doors and footsteps.

"Are you all right?" a voice asked.

Adam heard some mumbling. He heard other voices.

"Help! Let me out!" Adam yelled through the crack. He heard footsteps.

"Is someone in there?"

"I'm in here. Let me out," Adam yelled.

He heard a click and then the big door rolled up. Adam put his hands over his eyes to shield them from the bright headlights of the car.

"Are you all right, son?" a man in a suit asked.

"I'm ok," Adam said. "The driver of this truck tried to kidnap me."

"What?" the man asked in surprise.

"They stuck me in this truck back at the carnival in Lewistown." Adam walked around the side of the truck. "Only they're moving tonight to Centerville."

"You're just outside of Centerville now," the man said. "The fair is

supposed to open there later today. You say they tried to kidnap you?"

The driver was stumbling around in the road. The truck had smashed into a tree, right before a bridge over the Sleepy Eye River.

"That truck driver is drunk as a skunk," the man said. "You're lucky you both didn't end up in the river. He claims he saw two men in bright clothes pointing swords at him. He says they were standing right in the middle of the road. Imagine that. He really must have drunk a snootful."

"I saw two men," the driver slurred defiantly. "They were right there. Right there. They had big swords that glowed like they were on fire."

He pointed out at nothing in the middle of the road. The man looked at Adam and winked. Another car drove up. A man and woman got out.

"We'll need to call the sheriff in Centerville," the man said to Adam. "This truck isn't going anywhere tonight."

As the other couple came up to talk, Adam walked to the rear of the truck. He felt for the key around his neck. As he held it in his hands, he thanked the Prince of Kings for his sudden release from captivity. He watched the drunken driver swaying around in the road.

Another car was coming up behind them. Adam walked over behind the truck to get out of the way. That's when he saw the old red bicycle leaning on its kickstand in the back of the truck. Adam ran over to it.

"My wish did come true!" he said out loud. He climbed inside the truck and patted the handlebars excitedly. He hopped on the seat. Immediately, the old red bicycle glided out into the air and landed softly on the highway.

"I'm sorry I ignored you," Adam told the old bike. "I'll ride you wherever you want to go."

The Spirit Flyer began rolling down the highway, heading south, away from the truck and bridge. Adam knocked the kickstand up as the front wheel left the ground.

Behind him, the drunken driver was still mumbling about men with swords. The first driver to stop was explaining what happened to the others who stopped.

"And that boy over there was locked in the back of the truck," the man said. "He said he was being kidnapped by some people back in —hey, where is he?"

They all turned and looked. Down the road in the distance, they saw the faint glow of what looked like the taillight of a bicycle as it sailed up over the top of a tree and disappeared into the night sky.

# THE
# KEY TO
# FREEDOM
· · · · · · · ·

# 18

Adam held on as the old red bicycle sailed higher into the sky. The fresh breeze felt good on his face. The moon was bright and full. He sailed through the air high above the twinkling lights from occasional farmhouses and distant towns. Above him the canopy of stars seemed extra bright and deep.

"I wonder if a Spirit Flyer could take a person riding among the stars," Adam thought. The boy clutched the key happily, until he saw the dark chain of beads hanging around his neck. Adam looked around fearfully. For a moment he thought he saw the shadowy dark bars of the cage.

"Not again," Adam said fearfully. The joy he felt from the escape began to leak out of him like air out of a balloon. "I wish I could get away from those bars and these stupid beads."

No sooner had he wished than he saw a strange sight ahead. A large tractor sailed out of a cloud and crossed in front of the big full moon.

"Uncle Samuel!" Adam cried out. The old bicycle shot forward. In an instant he was flying alongside the big red tractor.

The old man on the tractor smiled in the moonlight. "I thought it was about time we met up again," Uncle Samuel called out. "Hop on board."

The old bicycle and tractor slowly stopped in the middle of the sky. Adam carefully climbed onto the back of the tractor. He sat on the wheel well. "What about my bike?" Adam asked.

"Your Spirit Flyer knows what to do," the old man said. Uncle Samuel pushed a lever and the tractor surged forward. Adam held on tight.

"How did you know where to find me at this time of night?" Adam asked.

"I didn't," the old man said. "But the horn on my tractor started blowing, and I knew I needed to investigate. As soon I got on and started the engine, away we went."

"You won't believe what has happened to me." Adam quickly told him almost everything since the train ride when he ran away. "Just now I thought my Spirit Flyer was taking me home maybe," Adam continued softly. "I know I need to apologize to Uncle Jacob and pay Benjamin back the money I took from him. Then I want to get back on the path, like the Prince told me. Do you think you can take me home?"

"Yup. We *are* going home," the old man said with a smile. Then he pointed in front of them. Up ahead, shimmering above the clouds was a golden shining palace that was so tall and broad Adam couldn't see where it ended. The boy gasped as the old tractor suddenly soared forward. Uncle Samuel reached down and picked up a golden key hanging around his neck on a thin golden chain. As soon as he lifted the key, the big golden doors of the palace swung open to welcome the riders.

"Uncle Samuel, this is some place," Adam whispered, looking from side to side as they entered the golden shining walls. Crystal light flooded the air with such intensity it almost seemed to vibrate.

"Is this the first time you've been able to see it?"

"I've only seen glimpses of it a few times," Adam said breathlessly. "This must be the Palace of the Kings. No other place could be this wonderful. But I've never been here before."

"You have been here, but you just didn't realize it," the old man said. "This is your true home, after all."

"My home?" Adam asked.

"Sure, this is the real home for all children in the Kingdom," the old man said with a glimmer in his eye. "We all have a place here. Someday we'll live here forever with the kings, going on new adventures and seeing new things. Living here is your true destination. You can be sitting here and doing things on earth at the same time. This is the resting place."

Adam took a deep breath. A smile crossed his face, and he wanted to laugh. "You know, I do feel like I'm at home in a way I've never felt before, even when I was home with Mom and Dad before the war. Can this really be my true home?"

"That's why it feels like home," the old man said. "Your other homes are a shadow of what it's like to really be home here in the dwelling place of the kings."

Adam smiled happily. Everything seemed perfect. In the distance down the great halls, he could see rooms and more rooms and a big table filled with food enough for a giant feast. Other large doors were shut, making Adam wonder what treasures or adventures lay behind them. The boy wanted to run and open them, but something held him back. Something still wasn't right.

"I wish I could go open some of those other doors," Adam said sadly. "But something's wrong. I feel like I couldn't move from this spot."

"That's one reason the kings brought us here for this visit," the old man said gently. "You need to use your key."

Adam looked down at himself. He saw the golden shining key on his chest. At the same time, he saw the dark heavy necklace of beads hanging around his neck. The weight seemed unbearably heavy and unpleasant. The dark beads were now the size of grapefruits. The boy looked up fearfully and saw what he hoped had gone away. The shadowy dark bars surrounded him once more, though they didn't seem quite solid.

"This is that necklace that the ghost boy gave me," Adam said sadly. "Only it got bigger. And these bars are back again. It's like I'm in a cage."

"He gave you misery beads," the old man said seriously. "Bitterness grows the longer you hang onto it, slowing you down under its useless weight. If they keep growing, they'll turn into bars that make you believe you're a caged animal, a prisoner. But the Prince wants you to be free on your journey."

Adam grabbed the shadowy bars. He pushed and pulled the freezing cold darkness, but he couldn't get a single bar to move, no matter how hard he tried. It even hurt his hands. Out of breath, he dropped his arms to his sides. He felt so weak, he dropped down to his knees. The weight of the necklace seemed so heavy that he wondered if he would ever be able to stand up again.

"I can't do it," Adam gasped. He rubbed one of the beads wistfully. His thoughts immediately began to turn sour. "I'm helpless. And hopeless. I knew there was something wrong with me. I knew there was some reason the kings didn't like me. Did you bring me here to make fun of me?"

"Not at all," a voice said. Adam turned around. His eyes opened wide when he saw a man dressed in royal robes, standing just a few feet away. Adam's first response was to bow before the Prince of Kings, which he quickly did since it is easy to bow when you're already on your knees. Uncle Samuel also bowed deeply and smiled. The Prince looked at Adam with concern and compassion.

"We have a boy here who hasn't learned how to use the key you've given him," Uncle Samuel said. "He's acting like a prisoner rather than a free man."

"I want you to be free, John Adam Kramar," the King Prince said, nodding his head. He passed through the bars and stood by the boy. He looked at Adam, reached down and took his hand. He lifted and Adam stood easily. The Prince looked at the dark, heavy beads hanging around Adam's neck. His finger lightly touched each one. As soon as they were touched, the beads changed into the dark links of a chain.

"It's the chain," Adam said in surprise. "I thought it was a gift at first when I got it from that ghost boy."

"The chains, the beads and the bars are all made of the same lies," the King Prince said firmly. "Some lies may seem like a gift at first. But your enemy uses the dark links to weigh you down and trap you like a prisoner again. Some links are made of fears about your parents, fears of death, fears of what people think of you. Other links are made of your anger and bitterness toward people who've hurt you, like your cousins or Mr. Fattooka."

"But I thought I was supposed to be free from the chain," Adam said desperately. "Why isn't it gone?"

"It stays because you choose to keep on carrying it," the Prince said firmly. "You must learn to let go of your bitterness and disappointments. If you chose, you can carry those burdens a long time. But they will be a great weight to bear. And if you let them grow in anger, the bars will grow and will become a prison. You will feel like a slave instead of a free citizen in my Kingdom."

"But it keeps coming back," Adam said angrily. Once again he pulled at the bars. A multitude of dark, hopeless feelings buzzed around him like bees as he struggled. "The chain isn't locked, but I can't get rid of it or the bars."

"Only I can unlock the chain to begin with, and only I can remove it if you choose to wear it again," the King Prince said softly. "But I gave you a key. You have it with you."

"The key?" Adam asked. Adam looked down at his chest. He saw the small golden chain that held a golden key over his heart. Adam picked it up. "I thought you only used this once, to free me from the chain."

"It's tragic that some people do use it only once or a few times," the Prince of Kings said. "That is your key of freedom and life. The key brings freedom from the chain and it will also open the doors of blessing."

Adam looked at the key in his hand. Once again he saw his name, John Adam Kramar. He turned it over. On the other side was one word. "It says *ASK*," Adam said, feeling confused. "I don't understand."

"That's how your kingdom key works," the Prince said. "You have all true kingdom power and authority as a child of the kings. But to use your key, you have to ask, just like you asked me the first time to free you from the chain."

"A person just holds this key and asks?" the boy said suspiciously.

"It's sad, but many children in the Kingdom don't have the freedom they want or the things they desire because they don't use their key and ask," the King Prince said. "Some are too proud to ask, some are ignorant, and some are distracted and deceived by the lies of the enemies of my Kingdom."

"It seems too simple," Adam said. "Are you sure that's all there is?"

"What do you wish me to do?" the Prince of Kings said.

"Take this chain off me," Adam said automatically, gripping the golden key in his hand. "And get rid of these bars around me."

"Do you wish to forgive your cousins for calling you names and hurting you?" the Prince asked. "If not, that means you secretly want to hold onto that link of chain. I won't remove what you really choose to keep."

Adam thought for a moment silently. He knew deep down that his cousins probably really did like him. And even if they didn't, he was tired of being angry about stuff that had happened weeks ago. "Yes, please take it off," Adam said. "I forgive them for hurting me."

Instantly, several of the dark links fell off the chain and disappeared into the air before they hit the ground. At the same time, several bars disappeared. Yet more bars and links of chain remained. "It's not all gone. Didn't I do it right?"

"The weight of your fears remains," the King Prince said gently. "Ask me to take your fears, your anxious thoughts, and I will remove them, every one."

"Take them," Adam said loudly. "I hate being afraid. I hate worrying about my mom and dad, wondering if they'll die or come back. I hate it. Please take it off me. Take them all off me. I'm tired of being afraid of what people like my cousins think of me. I just want to be who I am."

He squeezed the golden key again and the King Prince smiled. In an instant, several more bars fell away as links of chain fell to the floor.

"There's more," Adam said.

"You must forgive Mr. Fattooka and Dudley and the others who hurt you at the fair," the Prince said.

"But they lied to me," Adam replied. "That rat lied and made me work like a slave."

"Do you want to continue living like a slave because of a greater lie?" the Prince asked. "Let go of your anger and forgive those who hurt you and misused you."

"But they did illegal things," Adam said with a frown. "They broke the law."

"It's true they're guilty and have broken the law," the Prince said. "But I am their judge, not you. Their punishment belongs to me, not you. Release them to my hands, or you will stay in the cage that you've built intending to punish them."

Adam was quiet. He looked at the remaining bars and suddenly understood why they were surrounding him. He felt tears in his eyes. "But how can I do it? It's too difficult."

"Use my key," the King Prince said solemnly. "Just as I had mercy on you and released you from the punishment of your chain, so you should release them, in the freedom that's your gift. Do you trust me, John Adam Kramar?"

The boy held the key tightly in his hands. In a wave of confusing feelings, he suddenly found the freedom and power to let go of Mr. Fattooka and Dudley and the others. "I give them to you. You take care of that situation. I trust you."

Instantly, the rest of the links of chain fell off, and the dark bars disappeared. Adam took a deep breath. He felt so light and free that he looked down to make sure his feet were still on the floor.

"Wow!" Adam said with a smile. "You really did it. This is great!" The boy looked down at the golden key. The metal felt heavy, powerful and glorious in his hand. Then he looked up at the Prince. The Prince was smiling. The boy knew the key only worked because the Prince had granted what he asked.

"Thank you for helping me," Adam said softly. He bowed again before the Prince.

"It gives me great pleasure to free the children in my Kingdom from their fears and burdens," the Prince said with a smile. "Use your key as often as you need to. Ask me, and I will give."

The boy looked at the shining golden key in his hand, a precious treasure. Then he looked back at the Prince.

"Adam, I love you and like you," the Prince said. "All the children in my Kingdom must learn to grow. Sometimes you will fail, but I will never fail you."

Adam closed his eyes and let the promise of the Prince of Kings fill his heart. For a moment, he saw himself wrapped in the Prince's royal robes, covered with his goodness and love. The boy lost all sense of time as the Prince drew him near and held him.

Up ahead, the doors that had been shut suddenly swung open. The Prince smiled and nodded. Adam looked at Great Uncle Samuel.

"That's your room, I believe," Uncle Samuel said with a smile and a wink. "You go on, and I'll meet up with you later." Holding the golden key over his heart, Adam ran forward through the grand palace hall to see what was beyond the open door.

# ADAM'S
# ROOM
• • • • • • • •
# 19

**As Adam ran** through the large open doors,
he felt more free than he had ever felt. Soft music filled the bright air
like the perfume of flowers. The huge room he was in seemed very
unusual. It didn't have just four walls or even five, but several more. In
fact, he looked and he wasn't sure he could see all the walls. They went
on and on in different directions. And though the room was huge, it
didn't seem at all empty, but charged with excitement and adventure.
He knew he had to explore.

He stood up and ran to the nearest wall. This wall stretched out for
over fifty yards at least. Thousands of photographs and pictures covered

it like wallpaper. Adam hurried over to look. The photographs were all of him in different times and places, but they didn't seem like ordinary pictures. As he looked, they almost seemed to come to life. They didn't appear flat and two dimensional. They were deep and long and carried a wonderful sense of the present.

"What kind of pictures are these?" Adam asked.

In one picture, he saw himself at his old home with his mother and father and sister, playing catch with a baseball in their backyard. It was Adam's birthday, and he remembered it as being one of the happiest days of his life. He reached out and touched it, and something strange happened. Adam found himself back home, just like he was in that picture. He was playing catch again, and it was just like doing it over and yet doing it for the first time too. He couldn't explain the sensation, except that it was really fun. Not only that, Adam saw that the Prince was in the yard with them the whole time. Realizing that he had been there made the family's fun time together even more enjoyable.

"This is really great," Adam said to the Prince in his family's backyard. "I never realized you were here this day."

"It's my joy to be with you always," the Prince replied.

Adam stayed in that one place for what seemed like a long time, just throwing and catching the ball, talking and laughing, enjoying his family's company and the presence of the King. Not only could he see the Prince with him in his yard, he could also sense the presence of the Prince's kingdom and palace all around. When he was ready to go on, he turned toward the palace. Instantly he was back in the room, looking at the wall of pictures.

"Wow!" Adam said. "This place is really fantastic!"

He continued quickly along the wall. Every picture was about his life. Some were happy times. Others had been sad. Adam looked at himself at the train station, saying goodby to his mother. Then he saw the Prince standing next to them. Even though that had been a painfully sad time, from his palace home he could see deeper into that time and that made all the difference. The Prince had been there all along, and his Kingdom was always near. Knowing that filled the boy with a comfort and peace he couldn't explain.

"Wow," Adam said softly. "I've never seen anything like this."

Adam walked along, looking at the pictures. He cringed when he saw himself being thrown off the ramp into the mountain of slop. But this time he saw the Prince, standing in the middle of the slop pile right next to him.

"I didn't see you there before," Adam said with amazement.

"You were too angry to see deeper," the Prince said.

"I was furious," Adam said. He watched as he threw the dark beads from around his neck into the wind and as the bars grew up in the whirlwind to make his prison.

"There's that stupid ghost boy," Adam said angrily. "Can I get rid of him, like the chain? Can I make him quit bothering me? He says that we belong together. That he's me."

"The ghost slave is a shadow of the person you used to be before you became a citizen of the Kingdom," the Prince said. "He's made of memories, lies and darkness. He's not the new you at all. You changed when you came into my Kingdom. You're a new person. The ghost slave's only purpose is to confuse and defeat you."

"Defeat me? But how?"

"The enemy's only real weapon is to lie. If he can get you to believe a lie, then he has won an important battle. The sooner you defeat a lie, the better."

"How do you defeat a lie?" the boy asked.

"By knowing and speaking the truth. When you reject the lies of the ghost slave with the truth, he will have no power over you. The truth sets you free."

Adam walked further along the wall, looking at the pictures. He saw himself flying up into the night sky with Uncle Samuel and arriving at the palace. "That's what just happened." He paused. The wall stretched out before him. There were still thousands and thousands of pictures remaining.

"That's the future," he whispered in awe. He wanted to go forward and look at them, to see what would happen. More than anything, he wanted to see if he could find his parents, to make sure they would come home from the war. Adam tried to go forward and look, but he discovered the Prince standing in the way.

"Your family's future is in my hands," the Prince said firmly. He put his hand on the boy's shoulder. "Your parents are always safe with me. They have a place here in my house just as you do."

Adam looked back at the pictures he could see, the times he had already lived through. In every frame, he could see the Prince there, watching over him and his family, in happy times and sad. At that moment, he realized that everything would be ok. The Prince would be with Adam in the future too, just as he had in the past.

Adam looked down the wall at the thousands and thousands of pictures that remained, waiting for him. With a question forming in his mind, the boy turned to the Prince. Even before he asked, the King Prince answered. "Your journey on earth is rich and good and filled with the adventures I knew when I thought of you before I ever spoke the earth into being." The Prince waved his hand out at the wall. "These are just some of my wishes for you, my lovely son. You will discover and taste them in their rightful time."

Adam fell to his knees. He clutched the legs of the Prince of Kings, his heart overwhelmed with feelings and thoughts he could barely comprehend. Deep peace and awe filled his heart as he touched the hem of the glory of this wonderful man and King. He wasn't aware how long he knelt there. He had never felt so complete, so filled with joy.

The Prince lifted the boy to his feet. When Adam looked up at his face, the Prince seemed very happy. "I have great pleasure in giving gifts to those I love." The King touched Adam's cheek tenderly. Adam smiled. His touch made him feel pure and free.

"You are free," the Prince said, answering his thoughts. "And you have my purity and goodness in your life just waiting to be used. Every blessing is yours, at every moment, in every situation, no matter what happens, in joy or sorrow. From the beginning, I appointed many good works for you to walk in. And you will use my gifts, as your journey testifies on this wall. You will learn to be content, and you will learn to find the ways of peace and freedom as you complete your journey of wishes."

He pointed to the thousands of remaining scenes on the wall, the future he couldn't see. Adam looked with amazement as he slowly began to understand. His future was secure and waiting, like a present to be opened each morning of each day. The King would be with him every moment, watching over him.

"You really are with me, just like you promised," Adam whispered. "And someday, I'm coming here to stay."

"Of course, this is your room, the one I prepared for you."

"My room?" Adam asked. "This is my own room?"

He gazed around the wonderfully strange room. There were so many walls. Near the wall of pictures was a wall with thousands of doors, each a different shape and size. And on another wall, there were thousands of crystal windows with scenes beyond them. "What are those?"

The Prince of Kings smiled. He pointed, and one of the doors opened. Adam could barely keep himself from running over and going through the door.

"I don't understand," Adam said, looking out through the distant door. Something interesting was happening, but Adam couldn't even begin to describe it. He saw some people that he knew were his father and mother, and then there were lots of others. His father didn't really look old or young exactly, but he did look happy. His father smiled out at Adam and waved. Adam waved back. Then someone else who looked strangely familiar waved at Adam. This person wasn't really old or young either. Then Adam opened his mouth in surprise.

"That's me!" Adam whispered. The Prince nodded and smiled as the strange, wonderful door slowly closed.

"My family, they're all here too."

"Of course," the Prince replied. "All my children have their own rooms, but we are one family together too. Those doors are waiting to be opened once you arrive here."

"There are so many doors on just that one wall," Adam exclaimed. Then he gazed at all the other walls in his room. He looked and looked and looked some more, and he still didn't feel like he had begun to see what was to come. Finally, he took a deep breath. "Wow!" was all the boy could say.

The Prince put his hand on Adam's shoulder. He looked deep into the boy's eyes. The Prince pointed back at the wall with all the scenes and pictures of John Adam Kramar's life on earth. "All these days, this journey, is only a vapor on a summer's morning. When the sun shines, the vapor is gone and the day without end begins here in my presence."

Adam nodded, trying to take it all in. From where he stood, he could see way down the wall to where it began and all the way over to the last scene. But then he looked around the room and saw all the other walls and wonders that were waiting.

"It really is only a short time until we come here," Adam said.

"And death passes like a blink of an eye," the King Prince said, snapping his fingers.

Adam stared at the wall filled with the wishes of a king. Though he couldn't see the details, he knew a whole exciting journey was still ahead. And after that, in the palace, a thousand other walls and doors would open to journeys that would begin in their own time. With a secure sense of his true home waiting, the boy turned toward the Prince. Adam was ready to continue his journey.

"John Adam Kramar, you will overcome, because I've already overcome for you. Everything is prepared, everything is waiting for you."

"Thank you," Adam said gratefully. He dropped to his knees and bowed again. Then he stood up. "What's next?" Adam asked excitedly.

"I want you to remember this occasion while you are on your journey," the King Prince said. He pointed behind Adam. The boy turned around. There in the middle of the floor was a big red tractor. *Spirit Flyer Harvester* was written in flowing white letters on the side. Adam didn't even have to ask. He climbed up quickly and sat in the seat behind the steering wheel.

"This is just like Uncle Samuel's tractor!" Adam said excitedly. "How does everything work?"

"Your uncle and I will teach you as your journey continues."

Adam saw a slot for the key to start the tractor. Even before he could ask the question in his mind, he knew the answer. He took the golden key from around his neck and tried it. The key fit perfectly.

"Go ahead," the Prince of Kings said. "Your key was made to be used as often as you need it."

Adam turned the key and the tractor chugged into life. The boy smiled. Then a great sense of expectation came over him. He turned the key so the tractor became silent.

The Prince of Kings walked over and stood next to the boy on the tractor. "I have something I want to say to you," the Prince said seriously. "There are times in your journey when you and I will visit together in special ways. This is only one of those times. Even so, much will remain, many questions that can't be answered in full until your journey on earth is complete."

"I've got a million questions already." Adam looked at his special room. The King Prince nodded and smiled.

"I've given my children enough to go through their journey in my book and in the communion I have with them through the gifts of my Spirit," the Prince of Kings said. "When you read that book with the key of understanding, you will have faith and courage enough to travel over the times and situations that you don't understand. Someday, in this room, we will look at everything on your journey, and every question that remains in your heart will be answered to your complete satisfaction."

Adam nodded. Looking into his eyes, he realized he had never trusted anyone so completely as he now did this friend and King.

"This is a time for growth and new things." The King Prince pointed to the tractor. He reached up and placed his hand on Adam's head. Then he began to speak in a powerful, loud voice. "I bless you with all the treasures of my kingdom. You will be a teacher of many, a shaper of hearts, a fountain to those who are thirsty. To those who are lost you will carry my light. On your journey, you will help many children to be released from the dominion of darkness and the captivity of their chains. Your hands will distribute the gifts and treasures of my Kingdom."

Adam felt deluged, as if someone were pouring a huge tub of water over his head. The words covered him, pounded him gently and penetrated him inside and out, covering him like the royal robes that covered the Prince himself.

"From this point forward, I want you to be known as John, your first name, which means 'the blessed gift of the kings,' " the Prince said firmly. "The old Adam is gone, the new is come."

The Prince kept speaking, defining the boy in terms too wonderful to say out loud. As his hand lay on Adam's head, for an instant Adam saw himself turning like a piece of clay on a potter's wheel. With each word, he was formed and shaped just as the potter intended. The King Prince spoke the truth with such firmness that Adam would never see himself in the same way again, for he had been called and defined truly by the one had created him and given him life.

After the Prince was through speaking, there was nothing left to say. He smiled at the boy. John Kramar, the blessed gift of the kings, smiled back with a new confidence.

John Kramar knew what to do. He turned the golden key and the red tractor roared to life. He looked over at the chair where he had been sitting earlier when he first woke up in awareness of the King's palace.

Though he was sitting on the tractor, he saw himself sitting in that chair of blessing, resting securely in the knowledge of everything that the Kingson had already accomplished and won so long ago. In that instant, John realized that no matter where he was on his journey, his deepest wish would always be to return to this place, his true home with the kings themselves.

As the old tractor began to move forward, carrying the boy to the next adventure, John saw himself still sitting and resting in the chair. The boy smiled. He didn't know how the Prince could do it, but somehow the boy realized he would always be sitting in that chair, because this was his room and his true home. His best wish for each day to come had already been given to him once and for all.

# THE
# TRACTOR AT THE
# FAIRGROUNDS

• • • • • • • • •

# 20

The boy on the tractor continued his journey as he burst into the sky high above the clouds on a beautiful summer day. He held on to the steering wheel as the tractor glided down swiftly through the air. As they passed through the clouds, John saw the familiar sight of the Centerville courthouse. The tractor roared as it turned to the east toward the fairgrounds.

The tractor dropped lower in the sky. Down below in the fairground parking lot, he saw an old man sitting on another red tractor. Uncle Samuel waved at John. The boy on the tractor chugged down out of the sky, rolling to a stop by his great uncle.

"Look what the Prince gave me," John shouted, pointing at the tractor.

"This has been the greatest day!"

The old man nodded. "It's a real privilege to drive a Spirit Flyer Harvester," Great Uncle Samuel said, pulling his beard. "You've got a special calling on your life, son. The kings have chosen you to do some special things, things not everyone can do."

"How do you know that?" the boy asked.

"Because I saw it when you were born," Uncle Samuel said. "At Jacob's farm, you were the only one able to lift my staff. None of the others could pick it up. That means the Three Kings have made you able to carry responsibilities that others aren't meant to carry."

"I'm not sure I like that idea," John said with a frown. "Simon and all those guys think I'm scrawny and weak. What if they're right?"

"We all are weak," the old man said. "It's not our natural strength or ability or power. We rely on what the Prince of Kings gives us. He gives his ability, his goodness, his power and gifts."

More and more cars and pickup trucks pulled into the crowded parking lot. John noticed his Uncle Jacob's pickup truck parked nearby.

"Is Uncle Jacob here?"

"The whole family is here," Great Uncle Samuel said. "And your Spirit Flyer Harvester brought you here, so there must be a reason."

Just then, the horn on John's tractor began to blow. John looked worried. "What do I do?" the boy yelled out to the old man.

"Hang on and ride," the old man said with a twinkle in his eye.

The horn blew louder as the tractor began to move. John held on tightly as the tractor glided up into the air, turning toward the fairgrounds. The engine roared as it headed over the banner that read *Fattooka's Fantastic Midway*.

"He is here, just like I saw that day in the tree," John said.

People on the ground craned their necks to watch the old red tractor chugging along above them. "What kind of ride is that?" Benjamin Kramar asked his father as he looked up. Both of them stopped eating their cotton candy to stare. "Hey! That's a Spirit Flyer Harvester!"

John wasn't sure where the old tractor wanted to go. Then it happened. Up ahead, there was a loud popping noise and a bang as the spinning ferris wheel suddenly ground to a halt and lurched to one side.

"It's broken again," John said. Screaming filled the air as the buckets on the big wheel flopped and swayed. People on the ground ran in fear as the ferris wheel lurched and leaned over even farther.

John and the Spirit Flyer Harvester whooshed down out of the sky. He could see that no one was at the controls of the ferris wheel. Sparks and flashes of light shot out as the giant gears screeched in agony. John knew what he was supposed to do. The tractor slowed down as it glided up next to the broken ride. He stopped the tractor in mid-air, next to a blue bucket with three children inside.

"Hop on!" John yelled. The children carefully climbed out of the bucket, onto the back of the tractor. He flew up to the next bucket and the two children in that one climbed aboard the old red tractor too. Three more children climbed on from the next bucket. The tractor was full, so John guided it to the ground.

The children hopped off and ran to the arms of their waiting parents. As soon as they were safely off the old tractor John headed back up into the air. Bucket after bucket of children and adults climbed to safety on the back of the Spirit Flyer Harvester. John made four more trips to the ground.

On his way back up the last time, the ferris wheel groaned loudly again and suddenly began to fall. People everywhere screamed and ran farther back. The big tractor surged forward, heading right for the wheel. John blinked in surprise. The outer bar of the big wheel hit the hood of the tractor, snapping off the smokestack.

The tractor jerked so hard that John thought he would be thrown from his seat. But somehow he managed to hang on. The ferris wheel sparked, screeched, fell and halted on top of the hood of the tractor, which was parked solidly fifty feet up in the air. Several empty buckets on the ferris wheel snapped loose and fell to the ground. The huge wheel shuddered again, but the sturdy Spirit Flyer Harvester kept it from falling. Only two swaying buckets with passengers remained, and they were right next to the hood of the tractor. John was surprised when he saw that his cousins, Reuben, Simon, Jude, Dan and Joseph, were the last persons left on the wheel.

"Climb out on the hood," John called out. His cousins' faces were pale with fear as they climbed out on the rim of the ferris wheel. One by one they made their way to the hood of the tractor. John clutched the golden key in his hand.

"Keep them safe," he asked out loud as he watched them escape. Simon was the last one to leave the big wheel and step onto the hood of the tractor.

"Everything's clear," Reuben said. "Let's get out of here!" John nodded and pulled back the gear lever. The tractor moved backward slowly away from the ferris wheel. The wheel's metal scraped the red paint off the hood down to bare metal. Everyone held their breath as the rim of the wheel slipped free.

For a moment, everything was eerily quiet as the big wheel fell through the air. Then it hit the top of the food shack and crashed right on through it with a sickening crash. People on the ground began to cheer and clap. Others ran to put out a small fire that had started in the smashed food trailer.

John hit the gear lever, and the wounded tractor moved forward through the air. The old tractor chugged louder without its smokestack, but no one cared. John guided it down and landed softly in the parking lot near the fence of the fairgrounds.

His cousins yelled and whooped when the big wheels finally rolled to a stop. Until that moment they had been too scared to speak. But now they didn't have to speak, their eyes full of gratitude said it all. They slapped John on the back and hugged him. Even Simon hugged John.

"We've missed having you around the farm," Simon said.

"I've missed you guys too," John said.

"And I'm sorry about the way I treated you," Simon added. "Even if you hadn't just saved our lives, I was going to tell you that I'm glad you're our cousin. And I hope you can come stay with us on the farm again."

"Thanks," John said. He extended his hand and Simon reached out his own. The two cousins shook hands on their new friendship.

"We've got company," Reuben said. "Here they come."

All his cousins gathered around. John looked up as a crowd of people rushed toward the amazing red tractor which had saved the day.

# FEELING
# AT HOME
· · · · · · · ·

# 21

The next day, John and his cousins stood under a big shade tree by the workshop on Jacob Kramar's farm. Great Uncle Samuel was carefully welding a new smokestack on the hood of the Spirit Flyer Harvester. His own red tractor was parked under another tree nearby. Uncle Jacob and Reuben walked over carrying a newspaper.

"Uncle Samuel will have that tractor running like new," Jacob Kramar said with a smile. "Then you can get a proper picture for the Centerville *Gazette.*"

His uncle held up the newspaper. On the front page were several photographs of the near tragedy at the fairgrounds. The biggest photograph was of John sitting on the Spirit Flyer Harvester. John smiled at the photograph.

"They have a big story," Reuben said. "They arrested Mr. Fattooka and a lot of his workers. They found all sorts of stolen stuff in his trailer in big locked boxes. The sheriff said he'll be in jail a long time for the things he did. Everyone's amazed that no one got hurt on that ferris wheel sooner. He was warned to shut it down in several towns, but he kept making excuses and slipping away."

"They arrested that guy that crashed his truck into the bridge over the Sleepy Eye too," Benjamin added. "He confessed to driving stolen goods back east. He said he made a trip every two weeks. Did he really try to kidnap you?"

"That was the plan," John said. "But the kings rescued me, just like they rescued all those people on the ferris wheel."

Great Uncle Samuel stood up and took off his welding mask. He turned off the torch. "The kings had a great victory, all right." He patted John on the back. "And John, here, was wise to give them all the credit and honor. Thirty-two people in all were saved by the Spirit Flyer Harvester being at the right place at the right time. A great tragedy was prevented. The kings are to be thanked."

"John should take some of the credit, don't you think?" Simon asked.

"All I did was hold on to the Spirit Flyer Harvester," John said. "And for a while, I wasn't sure I was going to be able to even do that."

"You did fine." Great Uncle Samuel patted John on the back. "Really, all of us are riders. The kings gives us the awesome privilege of sitting in the driver's seat, but they make everything work. We play an important role, no doubt about it. We get to give away their gifts to others, but without the kings, we'd have nothing of true lasting value to give. The treasure and the honor all belong to the kings."

"It said in the paper that Goliath Toy Company may buy the midway since Mr. Fattooka's been arrested," Reuben said. "I never heard of Goliath Toy Company."

"What about Mary, her brother and the other kids that worked for Mr. Fattooka?" John asked.

"Mary and Danny want to stay here with us until they decide what to do," Uncle Jacob said. "And lots of people in town volunteered to take in the other children. Everyone was outraged when they learned about the way Mr. Fattooka had been treating those kids."

"What about Dudley?" John asked.

"He's on his way back to reform school," Uncle Jacob said. "The sheriff told me Dudley ran away from a reform school in New York three weeks ago. This time they'll be more careful. They found your wallet and returned your money."

"Great!" John said with a smile. "I can pay Benjamin what I owe him and pay you for breaking your tractor."

"I told you that the damage was really minor," Uncle Jacob said. "The wreck looked worse than the actual damage."

"Still, it was my fault, and you did have to put on a new smokestack," John said.

"There's some other good news too," Uncle Jacob said. "Some people in town are taking a collection to give you a reward. I heard they collected nearly a hundred dollars."

"Really?" John asked. "But the Spirit Flyer Harvester is the hero."

"You can't give money to a tractor," his uncle said with a smile. "So I think they'll give it to you."

"Well, I know what I'll do with it," John said quickly.

"What?" Benjamin asked.

"It's a secret," John said softly. "But I know someone who could really use it."

He looked at Mary and Danny sitting on the porch, snapping string beans and putting them in the basket. Mary looked up and waved at John. He waved back.

"I bet she and her brother would like a ride on your tractor," Uncle Jacob said with a twinkle in his eye. "That smokestack is fixed. I'd say that tractor is ready to continue the journey."

"Me too," John said confidently. He climbed up on the old red tractor.

He took out his golden key and turned it. The engine chugged content-edly. Sitting in the seat, he felt immediately at home. He closed his eyes and could see his room in the king's palace. He looked at the wall and saw the journey of wishes spread before him. The Prince of Kings was smiling, waving him on. John smiled back and opened his eyes.

"It's nice to really feel at home, isn't it?" Great Uncle Samuel said with a wink.

John nodded and grabbed the steering wheel firmly. "I'm going to enjoy this journey from here on out," John said boldly. He turned to his cousins. "You guys want to come with me?"

"Yeah!" they shouted and climbed eagerly onto the old red tractor. When they were all on, he drove over by the porch. Mary and her brother happily joined the others on the Spirit Flyer Harvester.

Getting everybody settled was a challenge, but no one complained. John pushed the lever forward and the old tractor began to roll. Mary grabbed onto John's waist as the big wheels left the ground. Everyone else laughed and giggled. John pushed another lever forward and they soared upward, straight over the roof of the barn.

"Where are we going?" Mary asked excitedly. John reached down and held the golden key.

"Let me ask," he said. He held the key and waited a moment. He smiled and pushed another lever forward. The old red tractor shot up into the skies through the clouds and climbed even higher.

"What's that?" Mary pointed in front of them. Everyone stared at the sight. Up ahead, shimmering in the light of the sun, two sparkling golden doors began to slowly open.

"Look at that palace!" Benjamin yelled out in surprise and glee. "And look at that man inside!"

"You haven't seen anything yet," John said with a smile. The old red tractor surged forward toward the Prince of Kings, whose arms were outstretched to welcome the riders for a visit to their waiting home.